# Zero D

# The Autobiography of
# a Very Special Cat

## Translated and interpreted by
## Misty Bridges Vaverka
## and Elaine Heckingbottom

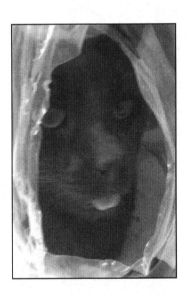

Dedicated to all those out there who are doing their part to show all animals that they matter – whether it be the vets and their staff who take care of them when they are ill; those who run homes, like Cat House on the Kings; or those of you who take rejected animals into your lives and into your hearts.

Particularly dedicated to Dr Brent and the other members of his team, who have done so much to help Zero and the rest of his zoo; also to the staff at the Earls Hall Surgery in the UK who did so much for Elaine's feline family, Scallywag and Raffles over the years.

Where would we animal lovers be without our vets and their staff?  Thank you for making a difference to animals like Zero Dark Thirty and the rest of the zoo. Here is his story!

All profits made on the sale of this book will go to help animals through charities such as Cat House on the Kings in California; Operation CATNIP in Stillwater, Oklahoma, Cats Protection in the UK, Battersea Dogs and Cats Home and other animal charities supported by our vets.

"Seek the opportunity to show you care. The smallest gestures often make the biggest difference." John Wooden

"Be the change you want to see in the world." Mahatma Ghandi

## Table of Contents

I am rescued.

You didn't care how I looked, or that I didn't have a pedigree.

You showed me that I am not disposable, and that I am worthy of love.

You brought back the sparkle in my eye and the shine in my coat.

You restored my spirit.

You took a chance on me just to see what I could become.

You gave me a place to call home, and a family of my own.

I am rescued.

# Chapter 1 - The Beginning

I remember one of my human family quoting the opening lines of a famous book one time. It went something like this: "It was the best of times, it was the worst of times." That more or less summarizes the weeks leading up to me finding a home with Misty and the gang.

One minute, I had a family, a home, someone who cared for me; the next moment, things were changing. I was homeless, unwanted, uncared for.

Everything had been fine until my first Mom had died and 'they' – the next people, her neighbors - had taken me to see a Man with Pointy Things because my tongue kept sticking out. No matter how much I tried, it wouldn't stay in – so they took me to get me checked out. And that was when the arguments began!

"So not just a black cat, which is unlucky enough, but one who's deformed! You heard him! Misaligned jaw!" the male voice growled. He had made it clear from the start that he didn't like me.

"He's cute, though!" the girl's voice put in.

"I don't care about cute. It's going to cost thousands of dollars to look after him – and where's that money going to come from? I'm telling you, this is for the best. Survival of the fittest and all that."

"But, Ben..."

"No. I've had enough of him!"

I didn't want to hear any more – it was too unpleasant, so I started to sing the song of my people to drown out the cruel words. But it didn't work – the next comment I heard involved the word 'caterwauling' and a very rude word that sensitive cats like me should never have to hear!

Suddenly, the car turned off onto a small country road and pulled to a stop. What was happening?

The car door next to me opened and my travelling carrier was unfastened. Was it a toilet break? Time for me to do my business? Eagerly, I jumped out of the car – after all, my little legs had been crossed for some time, and I had nearly had to resort to 'filing a complaint' in my box! I dived into the undergrowth to find a suitable spot but, as I did so, I heard the car doors slamming shut again. As quickly as I could, I did my business and reappeared … just in time to see the car disappearing back down the road. They'd forgotten me!

I meowed as loudly as I knew how, but nothing happened, so then I just sat there. Surely, they'd realize and come back for me? Looking around, I could see nothing – no cars, no houses – just trees, bushes and fields. What was I meant to do?

I cried piteously, but nothing happened. The song of our people has never been sung as forlornly as it was just then. I felt so alone.

I don't know how long I sat there, waiting for them, unsure what to do. It felt like days, but probably wasn't as long as that. I was starting to feel hungry and thirsty but didn't dare wander off: what if my family came back for me; how would they know where to find me?

It got darker and darker … I was beginning to feel cold, but I still didn't dare move. I must have sat there for hours until, finally exhausted, I curled myself into a tiny, miserable, jet-black ball and fell asleep.

Several hours later, as the sun was coming up, I felt a little nose pushing at me. I opened my eyes to find a tabby cat looking at me, curiously.

"What's up?" he asked me.

"I've lost my family … or, rather, my family have lost me." I told him, sadly. "I don't know what to do."

"You're not the first. You hungry?" he asked.

I meowed a pitiful "Yes". I was absolutely starving! I couldn't even remember when I had last eaten.

"Come on, then," he said. I started to follow, but then stopped. Where was he taking me? Surely this couldn't be good … and what if my family came back? How would they find me? He looked back at me. "Are you coming or what? They're cool people; they're real nice and they feed us. You'll be fine!"

Cautiously, nervously, I followed him down the road and into a small garden area with an open gate. There was a girl there; I remember thinking that she looked pretty – but I wasn't ready to trust yet. What I also noticed, though, was that there were a lot of cats there, and she talked to every one of them!

"Hello, Edward Enigma!" the girl called, putting down two bowls of food. "I see you've brought another friend for us today! I bet you're hungry too, little one!" I eyed the bowl cautiously. It smelt good and I really was very hungry, but I wasn't ready to trust yet ... not after what had just happened, so I just looked at it. She pushed it towards me, and I backed off a bit; but I didn't need to be scared. She could see that I was hungry and moved carefully away to watch me from a different part of the garden.

Edward lifted his eyes from his bowl briefly and looked up at me. His eyes seemed to say, "Come on, eat! It's good!" so I crept towards the bowl and started work. Edward was right – it *was* delicious – and I really was very, very hungry! Keeping a wary eye open towards the girl, I continued eating. She moved a fraction, and I started to back off; then she froze again. She clearly had a lot of experience with nervy animals. "It's alright, little one," she said, quietly. "Keep eating. I won't touch you if you don't want me to."

After I had cleaned the bowl better than any dishwasher, I moved back towards the gate to wait for my new friend, Edward Enigma.

"Goodbye, little one," the girl called. "I'll look out for you tonight when I come with the evening rations. I'm sure that Edward will bring you!"

Edward and I hung out for the rest of the day. I told him some of my story and he told me some of his. It was clear that he didn't fully trust humans – except the family that fed him - and, even then, it was obviously under his own terms. He showed me his favorite areas; but was happy to keep taking me back to the place where he had found me … just in case my family came back; but they didn't. There was no sign of them anywhere.

At supper time, we went back to the house, where the same girl welcomed me and pushed a plate of food in my direction. "Welcome back, little one!" she said.

Once again, there were a lot of cats around – and she talked to every one of them in a gentle, caring voice. I was still wary, but she stayed away and let me eat.

Day after day, I went back – usually with Edward Enigma, but sometimes by myself – and started to feel more confident. This family was nothing like the family who had rejected me. Then, one day, she said something that made me feel I could trust her.

"I just love the way your little tongue sticks out like that!" she whispered, pushing the plate towards me. "You are just so handsome!"

After I had finished my food, I moved over towards her. "Thank you!" I meowed at her, and she seemed to understand.

"You're welcome, handsome!" she replied. I moved a little closer, and she reached down with her hand. I was feeling brave and so I let her pet me. It felt different to my last family – kind of comforting. I couldn't help myself; I had to purr a little.

"You need to meet my Mom," she said to me. "She's going to love you!"

## Chapter 2 – Getting to Know You.

The following day, I went back again and, just like the girl had said, her Mom was there too, talking to all the cats who had come for food. With her was this strange furball – a rather obnoxious furball who seemed to have an awful lot to say for itself! Unfortunately, however, I didn't understand very much of what he was saying – he clearly wasn't talking my language.

It seemed a bit odd as, instead of the girl handing out rations, it was the woman who did it. She looked at me and I looked at her ... and the furball looked at us both. He still hadn't stopped talking loudly; he was clearly very excitable.

"Hush!" the woman said, bending down to pet him.

"Calm down, Biscotti Gotti! You're scaring our new little friend!"

But the truth is, I wasn't actually scared – it was more like curious. Edward Enigma seemed to get on OK with him, so he had to be alright really.

I remember that the woman sat down near me and just talked to me as I ate. I couldn't feel nervous of her – the girl was right about her; she was so gentle, and her tone of voice was so comforting. She seemed really nice! After a while, the girl came to join her, and they started to talk about me

"He's very cute - but a bit skinny, and certainly needs to eat more!" the woman said. "I reckon he needs a bath, and certainly a trip to Doctor Brent when he's ready, but he's the cutest thing I've ever seen! I just wish he would trust us a bit more!"

As we walked away, I asked Edward about the furball, and he told me a bit about him. Apparently, he was a puppy; no wonder I couldn't understand him! He'd been abandoned too; but had made a home with these humans a few months earlier. I decided that these were probably people that I could trust. I mean, seriously, if they let that obnoxious furball stay, they couldn't be all bad! But I still needed to think about it a bit more.

After that, I came back again and again for rations. Sometimes it was the girl, and sometimes it was the woman. Every day, at the end of feeding time, the girl would hold open the gate and look at me, urging me to stay; not to leave, but I wasn't ready to come in yet.

I was still trying to work out the furball, however – and it turns out that he was trying to figure me out too. Fortunately, it turns out that Edward Enigma is very bright and a bit of a linguist too – he had already learnt to speak 'Dog'. Over the next few days, he taught me enough to get by so, a couple of days later, said obnoxious furball and I managed a bit of a conversation.

"Where've you come from?" Biscotti Gotti asked.

"Not from around here," I replied.

"Well, duh! If you were from around here, Mom would have scooped you up already!"

"What are you?" I asked him, curiously.

"Duh! I'm a dog, and soon to be your bestest friend!" he retorted. 'Duh' was clearly his favorite expression!

"Friend?" I wasn't sure about that word. "What's that?"

"Duh! Don't you know that? A friend is someone that you play with, take naps with and share your toys with," he told me.

"Is Edward my friend?" I asked him.

"Well, sort of … but he likes to be on his own a lot.  But, right now you have a bestest friend; and not just any old bestest friend!  You now have a BFFF – a bestest furry friend fur ever!" he retorted.

"I think I might like to be your friend!" I said.

"That's good, because that's what I had already decided that we were!"  Biscotti Gotti retorted.  "Now, are you coming in, or what?"

"Maybe tomorrow!"  I edged away carefully.  I had taken a big step forwards today and wasn't ready for another one just yet.  Maybe sometime soon!  Who knew?


I kept coming back for rations over the next couple of days and kept being fed twice a day, every day; sometimes by the girl, sometimes by the woman - and sometimes Biscotti Gotti would be there as well, reminding me that he was my BFFF.

Every time, after we had all eaten, they went and stood by the gate, holding it open and I went out, back into the street.  Then, finally, I thought about what Biscotti Gotti kept saying.  He was my bestest furry friend fur ever.  If that was true, then I would have to trust these people – and they felt like people that I could trust.  And so, the next time she held the door open, I just sat there.

"Would you like to come in today?" she asked. I'm still not quite sure why, but I followed her up the steps and into my new life.

When the woman who was to be my new Mom and the boy who became my new human brother got home that night, they were astounded to see me sitting on the back of what would soon become 'my place'. Mom was the first to come over to me and start petting me.

"Well, aren't you just the cutest thing?" she told me. "I'm so happy to see that you decided to join us! We'll need to get you an appointment to see Doctor Brent, our vet, just to check that you are healthy."

I was a bit nervous about this – after all, I knew the word 'vet' was human speak for 'Man with Pointy Things' and my last experience of visiting one of these had resulted in that nasty argument, which had led to me being left behind, stranded!

"Brilliant!" barked my new friend, Biscotti Gotti, almost wagging his whole body in excitement. "You'll love our Man with Pointy Things! He always pets us and gives us lots of treats! Mom says that he's the bomb!"

That was the first time I'd heard that particular expression; but it was obviously a high commendation from my new BFFF, so I let it go.

I looked around. Was this what a family was supposed to be like? It was nothing like my first home. It was loud and filled with laughter; there seemed to be animals all over the place; and the person called 'Mom' was always smiling and telling everyone to be patient.

"Calm down, all of you," she chuckled. "I'm working on the rations – canine and feline first, then human. It's on its way!"

Could this be what I was looking for?

But, there again, if it was so perfect, why wasn't Edward Enigma inside with us? I stared out of the window, looking for the cat who had supported me through that tough first ten days or so, but he was nowhere to be seen.

Biscotti caught me looking and realized what I was doing.

"Edward don't come in 'cos he likes his freedom," he told me. "Mom says, if he ever decides he wants to come in, them doors are open; but he's lived alone for a long time, caring for himself. He's happy like that; inside life just isn't for him! But you – well, you're just gonna love indoor life. It's made for you! And don't listen to Arkham Darkham over there. It's not a prison. He just gets into more trouble than the rest of us and needs his time-outs. I mean *lots* of time outs." He looked at me again. "So now that we're BFFFs and you've moved in for real, what do you want to do first? I got a rubber chicken over there that could do with a bit of chewing ..."

I still wasn't quite sure what to make of it all; it was far more chaotic than I was used to – but, somehow, I was beginning to feel like I belonged.

Over the next few days, I met my other new brothers and sisters. Arkham Darkham was the first to appear, swatting me with his paw. I was soon to learn that this was one of his regular 'greetings'!

"So, you're our new brother, are you?"

"I think so," I replied.

"Hope you're good at mischief making!" he retorted, turning his back on me.

My first meeting with my brother, Emmett Alexander didn't go off quite so well.

"Why are you always sticking your tongue out at us?" he asked me.

"Why don't you have a tail?" I retorted, sharply. Clearly, I had hurt his feelings as he stomped off - but, then again, he had hurt mine too. It seemed as though we both had our sensitive areas!

Needless to say, we soon worked out our differences and eventually became quite good friends. No one can stay cross with anyone for very long in this house!

The two females of the family were harder to get to know. The family referred to Harley Quinn as The Ninja, as she was so good at hiding and creeping up on people, but she avoided me for the first few days. Garcia Maria Lopez, the other family dog, also seemed to keep her distance for a while ... until I woke up and found her napping next to me on Mom's bed and I had another instant best friend. She's a great nap buddy and a really caring friend.

As for my other new brother, Jasper Po, he was just so calm and relaxed. Nothing seemed to ruffle him at all.

"So, another brother! Cool!" he purred. "You'll love this family! Crazy, but totally cool!"

Just like that, I had been absorbed into the family and made to feel like I belonged. From feeling like I was nothing, I now had a place to call home again. Everything was looking good!

## Chapter 3 – The Man with Pointy Things

I had been inside for several days when, suddenly, the day that everyone seemed to have an opinion about finally arrived. I'd kept hearing things like 'vet' (from the humans), 'Man with Pointy Things' (from my new furry friends), 'check-up', 'mouth' – what was going on? I was really confused to start with ... and then rather worried because I saw IT! The carrier! OK, so it was different from the other one - softer and more comfy-looking - but it was still a carrier! I looked around in panic but, as ever, my new BFFF, Biscotti Gotti, was right by me.

"What's ya looking at?" he barked, curiously.

"I ... I thought they were keeping me!" I stammered, nervously.

"What d'ya mean?  Of course they're keeping you!  You're my new BFFF!  They can't get rid of you now!"

"So why have they brought ... that?" I asked, still staring at the dreaded carrier in confusion.  My last family had put me in one of those ... and they hadn't kept me – so what did it mean?

"Duh, you have to ride in the carrier to go in the car!" Biscotti retorted.  I was no clearer.

Arkham Darkham was on hand to help out.  "Dude, you go in the carrier to the Man with Pointy Things," he drawled.  "You take a little nap and you wake up less of a man.  And as long as you don't mess with your business, you don't have to wear the special hat!" he finished, sarcastically.

Even more confused, I looked at Biscotti Gotti.  "What's he talking about?"

"Well, basically you go in the car and you drive along and bark at other cars.  Oh, but you haven't learnt to bark yet – so I guess you'll just meow at them.  When you get to the place, Mom takes you out and they give you a bath and a haircut and sometimes a blueberry facial!  Ooh and sometimes you get to play with your other friends!" Biscotti explained, excitedly.

"Dude, he's not going to get gum removed from his butt because he was stupid enough to sit in it!" Arkham tried to explain to my over-excited friend.  "Mom's taking him for the other thing – the thing where she leaves with lots of papers and jewelry for us."

Jasper Poe was much more chilled. "Relax," he told me. "We all go there. You'll be fine. Oh … and don't forget to bring back the treats for us all!" He curled back up into a ball and went straight back to sleep. As for Harley Quinn, well, she was no use at all. In typical ninja style, she was in hiding.

I was very confused, and clearly Biscotti was too.

It was time to go, but this time it was different. Mom put my special blanket, the thing she called my 'woobie' in the carrier, because she said I would probably want it later.

I looked at Biscotti, fearful of what was happening, but he just said, "See ya later, pal!" and went to sit on the stool by the window, gazing into the distance

The next thing I knew, I was lifted into the carrier, taken out to the car and we were driving.

We came to a very different building from the last one owned by a Man with Pointy Things. This one looked more like a house than a clinic. Mom lifted me out of the car and took me inside, talking to me all the time.

"You'll be fine, little one; and I'll be back to get you before you know it!" was one of the things I remember hearing her say – something that gave me courage to face the inevitable.

Inside, it was loud and busy - and there were lots of other animals there. Dogs, cats, rabbits, guinea pigs – all sorts of critters. There was lots of room for waiting, but Mom didn't go to one of those places. She took me straight to the front desk, where she talked to a lady who looked into my carrier.

"What a cute little kitty! What's his name?" she asked.

Suddenly, I realized that I didn't remember my name from before. I'd been called so many nasty things by 'him', the man called Ben – brat, nuisance, and some that were even meaner; and then recently it had been cutie, little one, puss, kitty and sweetheart. What was my real name? I started to panic. If I didn't know it, how would Mom? Then, suddenly, I heard my Mom say, "His name is Zero. He was dumped as if he were nothing, but our Zero is going to be amazing. This is Zero, our hero!"

The new lady wrote something on her form. "Zero it is, then!" she declared.

Mom looked into my carrier and said "Alright, my little friend, I will be back later. You are in a great place. They will check you over and look after you."

She turned to the other lady and there were words like 'neutering', 'checking his mouth out' and 'for sure a flea pill'!

She reached into the carrier and petted my head. I pushed it further into her hand, all my heart crying a silent plea – "Don't leave me! Don't leave me!" but she couldn't hear me. She handed me to the new lady.

"See you later, Zero!" she said.

Zero! I had a name! And, if I had a name, perhaps I belonged!

Maybe this trip to the Man with Pointy Things wasn't going to be all that bad!

## Chapter 4 - Coming Home

The Man with Pointy Things, Doctor Brent, was very gentle. He petted me and spoke to me gently; then I felt a little prick in my paw. Before I knew it, I was asleep.

The next thing I knew, I was being woken up and carried into another room. To my surprise, Mom was in there, waiting, sitting in a little corner. The nice lady from before handed me very gently to Mom.

"He's been such a good boy!" she said. "He's a really lovely cat!"

"Is it time to go home again?" I wondered. I really hoped so. The people here were nice, but they weren't what I had begun to think of as 'my people.'

The man who carried several weird things around his neck and in his pockets (including pointy things) came in too. I remember that he had glasses on and was wearing a funny green top. He petted me gently and told me what a good boy I was.

"I've had a good look at him, Misty," he assured my Mom. "There's nothing really wrong with his mouth – except he's missing a few teeth - and, for some reason, his jaws just don't line up right – probably from birth. That's why his tongue sticks out like that. He needs to eat a few more good meals, and vitamins are an absolute must – other than that, he's perfectly healthy. You found a good one there!"

"I didn't find him," Mom replied. "Edward Enigma did! And somehow, he just seemed to belong!" She kept petting me too. Biscotti Gotti was right about that – visiting the Man with Pointy Things meant lots of petting.

Hang on a second, though! Although I was still somewhat groggy, I was sure there was something else my BFFF had said ... yes ... that was it! Treats! Where were the treats?

Sure enough, the Man with Pointy Things went straight over to the table in the middle of the room – where there was a huge jar of pet treats! He grabbed a paper bag and started filling it... and I mean *filling* it! I remember thinking "This man might have some fairly strange pointy things, but he sure is generous!"

"He'll want some of these when he comes to fully," he said, "and the rest of the zoo will never forgive me if you don't take enough for them all!" He passed the bag to Mom. "Make sure you give a few to Edward Enigma with his rations. He's earned them for looking after this one!" He paused for a second before adding, "When will I finally get the pleasure of meeting him?"

"Edward? When I can persuade him to trust me enough to allow me to bring him to you!" Mom replied. "He is one feisty cat, who absolutely detests indoors and fights any thought of being trapped."

"One day – and the sooner the better!" Dr Brent replied. "Cute and helpful though he may be, we really don't want any 'little Edwards' finding their way to your zoo!"

Mom smiled as she put the treats in her bag and placed me carefully into the carrier. "Come on, Zero!" she said. "It's time to take you back home. Biscotti Gotti is already missing you like crazy!"

Home! Even though I was still groggy, I realized that I had one – a real furever home – and I wanted to go back there. I decided, then and there, that this was my family and I was part of theirs. No one was upset because I was different; in fact, no one in my new family treated me any differently from anyone else. However, what I did realize was that someone really needed to be in charge of all the chaos, and I guessed that someone would have to be me. Or, perhaps it would be me ... once I wasn't quite so sleepy.

With that, I drifted off to sleep again, and knew nothing more until I woke up at home, still in my carrier, but with the door open – and there was a half destroyed stuffed toy waiting for me. Mom was right. Biscotti Gotti clearly had been missing me!

It was clear that my new life had really begun. I had a home, I had a family and now I even had a name. Zero.

# Chapter 5 - My New Job

The days that followed were interesting.  I had never had so much fun!

I sat and watched as Biscotti Gotti destroyed every single toy Mom gave him.

---

Mom: What are you doing, Biscotti Gotti?

Biscotti Gotti: Duh, Mom!  What does it look like?  I'm taking out this stuffed animal.  I told it I would be back later - well, I'm back!

Mom: Do you really have to destroy it quite so thoroughly?

Biscotti Gotti: Don't worry.  I know what I'm doing.

I've taken out a good many stuffed animals.

Mom: (with a sigh) Oh, Biscotti Gotti. You really are such a hot mess!

I watched Arkham Darkham stir up trouble, resulting in loads of time outs (usually in comfy places, which sort of defeated the object) and, occasionally, I glimpsed my furry sister, Harley Quinn. She was a bit like a ninja; I never knew when she would turn up! I made friends with Garcia Maria Lopez during nap times and made up with Emmett Alexander.

On my first outing outside, I realized that I had never really looked around the enclosed area. Turned out that it was rather nice! There was a fantastic looking dog house – I was told that it was for Edward, or anyone who needed a warm, dry place to sleep when it got cold. There was a table with a giant umbrella which, when it was opened, made a cool, shady place to nap on hot days. And then there was the garden! It was full of flowers – both real and fake, because some flowers aren't safe for animals and, believe me Biscotti Gotti will eat anything!

But the thing that I found in the garden which I really loved was the birdbath. It was perfect! I could rule my new kingdom and take a nap at the same time! I remember, when Mom first saw me sitting in it, she looked at me fondly.

"It's like you're a little ruler on your throne!" she said. "Good luck, keeping this zoo together!"

I realized that it was quite a job to take care of all my family. Emmett Alexander 'filed complaints' quite regularly, in a variety of places – under the table; in the bath; in a shoe – anywhere except in the litter box; but they almost never reached me or Mom for one, simple reason: Biscotti Gotti! He eats literally almost everything, no matter how gross; and any 'complaints' left anywhere other than in the litter tray were regularly disposed of in this way! Can you believe it? He might be my BFFF, but that dog is weird!

Another problem with Biscotti was not so much the fact that his favorite thing in all the world is digging – that's actually great! The real problem was that he was easily distracted, which meant that he would start a hole, then something would happen, so he would totally forget that he had ever started a tunnel. It could be so frustrating at times.

Edward still came and went, and I was still confused as to why he didn't want to live inside with us. I asked him again one day.

"This is the life you were always supposed to have – inside," he told me. "For me, I like it outside. I have places to stay when it's cold or it rains and, occasionally, when it gets really cold, Mom will force me inside for a bit – but she knows I'm not happy when she does that.

Yes, I know they love me, and I love them – in my own way. Mom always makes sure I have food and water, so I have what I need. Besides, if I were inside, how would I help cats like you who have no idea how to survive?"

"That's true! I would very probably be dead by now if you hadn't helped me!" I replied. I would always be grateful to Edward Enigma for helping me when I was lost, but I was still a bit confused.

"Exactly. We both have our jobs to do. Mine is leading the lost – but yours is something very different."

"You really think I have a job?" I asked

"Well, yeah! We all have a purpose. Mine, as I say, is leading the lost; some of us just provide comfort – which is very important in its own way; for others, their job is to be friends – and, again, that's important. Yours, I can already tell, is different from all of those. Yours is to start a revolution!"

"A revolution? Do you really think I could be a leader?" I was beginning to like this idea.

"Sure. You already have your kingdom. Now, you just have to figure out how to get other people to join!" Edward answered

With Edward's encouragement, I decided that I really did have a purpose. First and foremost, it was to take care of my family but, secondly, I knew that Edward was right. There were a lot of animals that needed rescuing – just like me.

The world needs a revolution, and I am the cat that is going to lead it – with the help of a few humans, some dogs and some other cats!

Zero's revolution! I smiled to myself. I liked the sound of that one!

## Chapter 6 – Learning to be a Dictator.

The days turned into weeks.

My days were filled with tunneling, along with overseeing my new kingdom. Arkham Darkham, always the mischief maker, kept me on my paws. Biscotti Gotti continued to have a love/hate relationship with rubber chickens, stuffed toys and dolls. They rarely survived very long. My other feline brother, Jasper Poe, didn't seem to have a care in the world, and my (slightly) purry sister, Harley Quinn, just hid wherever she could!

Before long, I was given a second part to my name, just like all my other furry brothers and sisters. For a while, I had been a bit worried about only having a single name – I was concerned that it might mean that I didn't belong properly yet - so I asked Mom about it.

Me: Mom, can I ask you something?

Mom: Zero, anything – you know that.

Me: Well, all my brothers and sisters have more than one name. Biscotti is Biscotti Gotti; Arkham is Arkham Darkham – and, as for Garcia, she has three names, Garcia Maria Lopez – but I am just Zero. Why?

Mom: You're not 'just' Zero. Zero is a very special name. We chose it for you because it showed that you were left as nothing – but you were far, far more than that. You are Zero, our little hero!

Me: Yes, but what's the rest of my name? Do I have another part to it?

Mom: Well, we had to wait for that bit till we really knew you – but it's obvious now. You are Zero Dark Thirty.

Me: Zero Dark Thirty? I like that! Why did you pick that name?

Mom: Zero, it was so obvious when you got to know you. That's the time of day when you do all your best plotting!

Me: Prrrrrr!

So, I wasn't just Zero anymore; now I was Zero Dark Thirty! I was very proud of my name – particularly because of the reason why Mom chose it! Great choice, Mom!

There were holidays and birthdays. Time seemed to move on; I was happy and so very much loved.

Some days, we were really busy; up to mischief all over the place – particularly in the garden. It didn't take me long to decide that the bird bath was mine – although it took me a while to apprise some of my brothers and sisters to that fact! On other days, I woke up and decided I wasn't moving. Mom's bed was far too comfy! That's those therapeutic mattresses for you! Plus, some days it was just far too hot to move! It wasn't as if we were going to get any yard time on days like that, anyway.

Some days, I was happy to be at home, where I was safe and protected and where my family cared for me and loved me; but, at other times, I was jealous of Edward Enigma's freedom, and wanted that for myself – the freedom to explore more of the world; so, I kept plotting and planning. How could I escape? How could I get out there? And would I still be able to get back in when my adventures had finished? Jasper Poe kept telling me to relax; all was fine - but I couldn't help it. Part of me wanted to be out there so, when I saw how well the others could dig, particularly the dogs, I was keen to rally my troops!

Most days, however, I saw how comfortable we all were; how well our human family looked after us and how much they spoilt us; and I was more than happy to stay where I was. I hate to admit it, but Edward Enigma did good when he brought me here. He clearly knew what he was up to!

## Getting to know my family better

Before long, I began to learn everyone's history as well as their strengths and weaknesses.

- Jasper Poe:

Jasper was the first member of the current family to be adopted – in fact, Mom often says that he actually 'chose' them by reaching out his paw whenever Mom and Nana passed his little cage.

Mom was mourning the loss of our sister, Bella Marie and had not been intending to get another cat at the time – but Jasper had other ideas! He always said that, as soon as Mom and Nana walked in, he knew they were his furever family, so he just had to say 'hello.' Apparently, it was love at first sight – he came home that day!

He was definitely the calmest out of all of us, not easily angered or ruffled - but prone to singing 'the song of the people' at very strange times.

- Emmett Alexander:

When my human sister first saw him, he was a tiny kitten with a tail that was a mangled mess. It turns out that the humans he lived with had tried to bob it – with a pair of scissors! Even Doctor Brent couldn't save it – which left him with a cute little bob. However, his lack of a tail never held him back – he seemed to be able to balance quite easily; especially when catnip was around!

He was also incredibly good at distracting the humans, making them forget what was going on. He was a purrer, and the humans loved it.

He and Jasper Poe were BFFFs and often snuggled together – particularly in cold weather.

- Harley Quinn:

When she first arrived, I was told that Harley Quinn was a tiny little thing who hadn't even been weaned; and she had an awful eye infection. Doctor Brent had been worried that he wouldn't be able to save her eyesight; but he performed his usual magic and now she's heathy, with beautiful eyes and perfect eyesight.

Mom always called her a ninja because she could be incredibly stealthy and would literally appear out of thin air. One minute she would be there and the next, she was gone. Talk about Houdini!

I soon found out that a game that the humans liked to play was one they call "Where in the world is Harley Quinn?" Sad to say, Mom was not very good at this game, bruhahaha! (my evil laugh!) Harley Quinn could stay hidden for as long as she wanted – or at least until ration time!

- Arkham Darkham;

He may be cute looking, but he was actually the Master of Mayhem and our resident mad hatter. From the time he would hit the floor no one was safe; Arkham Darkham was an equal opportunity prankster.

He had been adopted by a group of students from the local town; but they soon found out that he was too much for them, so Mom brought him home, and fell in love with this hot mess – her first foster failure!

If you think you are in trouble, just wait for it. There it is, the human called Mom is yelling his name! Whatever you have done, you can almost be certain Arkham Darkham has done something worse. Also, I feared, ADHD might be named for him – Arkham Darkham Hyperactive Disorder! He finds it hard to keep his paws to himself and is usually the first to cause chaos or mayhem.

Mom reckons that Arkham Darkham actually taught her counting. Yes, she counted whenever he was doing something he shouldn't be, and yes, he learned that, when she got to 3 it was a time out! She often said that, if the Energizer Bunny ever ran out of energy, they could give her a call and borrow Arkham Darkham!

- Garcia Maria Lopez:

My lovely sister from another mister was found in a ditch, half frozen, and taken to the local rescue center, where Mom and my human brother and sister found her. My human brother fell in love with her straight away, and so she became the first canine member of the family. It took a while for her to learn to trust but, once she felt safe, she became a very loving member of the family.

However, although she could be a good nap buddy, there were times when she seemed incapable of sitting still or being quiet for long periods of time; and she was very nervous of strangers – particularly male strangers. Mom was sure that she had been abused during her short life.

Her main strength, however, was that she was the best hole-digger around!  Need a hole digging?  Garcia Maria Lopez is your woman!

- Biscotti Gotti:

Apparently, this little dog – not much more than a puppy - was first found running around the area in the road by our house just a few months before I turned up.  I'm told that it was pouring with rain and he was covered in mud, very wet and running in the road.  Mom tried to get him, but he ran! Honestly … he often said that, if he'd known about the rubber chickens and kaboobles on offer, he would surely have stayed put and let himself get caught!

It took a few more days for my human brother, the family athlete, to catch him and bring him home … and that was it! Biscotti Gotti had a new home, and our home had a new hitman! Seriously, the number of soft toys, dolls, rubber chickens etc. that he destroyed had to be seen to be believed.

Mom always reckoned that this picture summarized him. If you ever needed a stuffed animal taken care of, or perhaps its eyes removed he was your guy.

As far as I was concerned, Biscotti could be highly unstable. Mom said it was because he was a puppy; I said it was because he was crazy! However, he had his strengths as well and was one of the most loyal friends that you could ever hope to meet.

- And then there was me: Zero Dark Thirty. Instigator, plot creator, overall master of mayhem! The newest member of the family but, basically, the ring-leader of the gang; the one with lots of plans. Bruhahaha!

These were my fellow prisoners; my very own suicide squad! This is why I clearly made little to no progress in my plans for escape!

There was also a slew of feral cats who came for regular rations, just as I had done in the beginning. Some of them came and went; others were regulars. Edward Enigma was definitely their leader and looked out for them, just as he had done for me. It still confused me that he never came in, but it was something that I clearly was going to have to learn to accept.

Then there were the humans: our Mom, our human sister, Hayley, and our human brother, Jax; not forgetting Nana and Pops, who popped round regularly – all great for cuddles and treats; and Jax could be a good partner in crime at times too!

## The start of the diary

Mom and I kept talking to one another at night, and we decided to create a diary together – Zero's Secret Life – and post it on Cat House on the Kings, the Facebook page of a fantastic no cage, no-kill, non-profit cat sanctuary in California that she supported. We couldn't believe it when we realized that our entries were being read, laughed at and commented on, not just by Mom's friends but by people all over the world! The revolution had begun.

Mom and Elaine kept re-reading these diaries as they put this book together. They said it was 'invaluable' – I really hope that's not the opposite of 'valuable'!

# The Mystery of the Smurf Village

I'll never forget the day when I was convinced that I had found the missing Smurf village!

It wasn't very long after we had been sitting together on the sofa alternately watching the film 'Smurfs: The Lost Village' and dozing, when I spotted _it_! For around five seconds, I felt like the cat Azrael from the film – even though I was the wrong color. I had found the missing village! It was right out there, in front of me, in the area outside our garden – lots of little, creamy-white Smurf houses! It was as if they had just appeared overnight! I gazed in awe. Who could I tell? Surely, this needed to be reported properly in the human's newspaper?

Suddenly, as I was standing there, staring at them, it seemed as though Mom was losing her mind! Without warning, I found myself being picked up and held firmly in her arms as she started kicking the little houses over.

"Don't touch them!" she shouted to us all. "They're dangerous! Stay away!"

I honestly began to think that she was going crazy! How could Smurf houses be dangerous? I meowed, trying to express my worries. What could I do?

Just as quickly, our yard time was cut short as she took me back inside, telling me not to worry – it would all be alright, then running out to get the others. But what else could I do but worry? It was in my nature! Those poor Smurfs! If I were them, I would be lodging 'complaints' somewhere outside the litter box; after all, I was convinced that they were now homeless, thanks to my Mom. She had completely wiped out their village!

I wondered where they would live now? Not in our house - it was already a bit of a zoo. Plus, I was fairly certain Arkham Darkham or Biscotti Gotti would eat them, given half a chance!

Nevertheless, for much of that night, I worried about the poor, homeless, Smurfs and where they would be sleeping. After all, unlike most of the others, I knew what it was like to be really and truly homeless. After a while, a thought came to me: perhaps they were in Edward Enigma's cold weather house – that funny dog kennel in the garden? That thought gave me a little peace and allowed me to rest for a while.

The next day, when we were back in the yard, the neighbors seemed unhappy. They asked my Mom, "Why did you cut those mushrooms down? We were letting them grow!"

Mushrooms? Human vegetables? So, it wasn't a Smurf village after all? Part of me was quite relieved at that news – at least I didn't have to worry about homeless creatures!

My mom, however, raised her hand. She was quite cross with our neighbors – which isn't like her, really. She doesn't lose her temper very often.

"I'm going to stop you right there," she replied. "Those 'mushrooms' out there are not edible. If you had actually eaten them, they would have done you no good – in fact, they would have made you sick, or, if they had got there first, would have made one of these animals sick."

Our neighbor's response: "Oh!"

My Mom's sarcastic remark as she was carrying me back inside was on the lines of, "Yeah, oh!" She then muttered to me, "Those people should really get their own human to make sure they don't eat things they shouldn't!"

I don't think that was the end of the story, though. A couple of days later, I saw Mom having another discussion with our neighbors. She was holding Biscotti Gotti and looking rather vexed … and yet more of those mushrooms had been knocked over.

Maybe they really did need to get someone to tell them what is safe to eat! As for Biscotti Gotti, it's a concern – he really does need to start thinking about what he eats!

# The Eclipse

One day, there was huge excitement in our area. Apparently, there was going to be something called an eclipse. The sun was going to be hidden behind the moon and everything was going to be dark for a while ... in the middle of the day.

My human family and their neighbors seemed to be really excited, as were the dogs (but, there again, that was nothing unusual: they got excited about everything!) Everyone was standing outside, all the humans wearing strange glasses and staring at the sky whilst the dogs carried on as usual. My feline siblings were out there as well, rolling in catnip and sniffing the flowers; and Harley Quinn was in one of her usual hiding places.

I wandered out and took a brief look. It was a bit strange seeing the sky get darker so early in the day but, seriously? I had better things to do with my time. A lot of fuss about nothing! Cats, particularly black ones, don't need to watch out for the supernatural; and Mom's therapeutic mattress was calling me much more loudly that this so called 'eclipse'. After all, her mattress is supposed to be very good for my back and, boy, is it comfy – particularly when it's all mine!

It's really great when nature distracts the rest of the family!

## White Icing!

Then there was the day that my brother, Biscotti Gotti, and I found ourselves in big trouble – and I mean REALLY big trouble! You see, it went something like this:

We might have found some white icing in the kitchen.

We might have, sort of accidentally, gotten some of said icing on my head and in the dog's beard.

Oops! Perhaps that might mean we were going to be in a major time out!

Mom might have had to cut some of Biscotti Gotti's hair because it had hardened like glue – and, worse still, I might have had to have a bath to get it off my head!

Seriously, I had never heard the word "No" so many times or in so many different volumes. Plus, I really began to think that our mom was going crazy. She kept talking to herself as she cleaned us up, asking herself questions about our current predicament. I think the dogs finally realized that we really must escape to avoid these impromptu cleanings.

By the way, I have to say that it was not really time out, lying on a therapeutic mattress. Mom really needs to rethink our jail time!

A couple of weeks later, Mom had our Nana drop Biscotti Gotti off for his regular grooming appointment. To her shock, when Mom picked him up, he was bathed ... but not trimmed! Apparently, his stylist prefers to work with hair that is all the same length and, equally apparently, cutting frosting out of beard hair is considered inappropriate!  Mom was not impressed.

I hated to break it to Mom but, just hours later, our human sister had to cut our human brother's chewing gum from Biscotti Gotti's butt hair because he sat on some – not the first time, and certainly not the last time he would ever do it!  At that rate, he was clearly going to have a wickedly wacky hair-cut for a while!

Still, at least he smelt April-fresh after his grooming session ... for a few hours, anyway!

## Night Time Shenanigans and Their Aftermaths!

I mentioned earlier that Jasper Poe likes to sing the song of the people: well, there were several nights in a row when he decided to do just that, both loudly and proudly at two in the morning, keeping us all awake.  Sometimes, it was for no real reason but, at other times, it was to serenade his lady-love, Columbia, who lived next door.

And he wasn't the only one!  Emmett Alexander has been known to sing similar songs for his own reasons – always in the early hours of the morning; and Arkham Darkham is another one who enjoys waking us up at weird times.  In his case, I fear it's out of pure mischief – on top of what I am sure is ADHD!  Seriously, can't they medicate for things like that? I know they do with humans – but perhaps Arkham Darkham Hyperactive Disorder is not well known amongst vets.

Whatever the problem, we certainly ended up with a few sleepless nights over the months. I don't really know what coffee is but, if it helps my human family after nights like those, I sometimes feel that we should all try it – either that or get ear-plugs! Do you think they make earplugs for cats … or even cat coffee?


One day, at our morning ration time, our Mom was so tired that she appeared zombie-like and, instead of our normal cat food, we all got kibbles and bits for breakfast! When our Mom realized what she had done, did she correct her mistake? Nope, she said we could all be dogs for one morning! Clearly someone should look into the management of this establishment. However, I have to say that kibbles and bits are quite good if my empty food bowl was anything to go by!

It just concerned me the way that Mom kept talking to herself! I'm sure I once heard someone say that was supposed to be the first sign of madness!

As I often say, fight the establishment!


Another day, she was so tired that she totally forgot what she was doing! You see, on a typical morning, she usually has two jobs on the go at the same time – one involves peanut butter; the other involves cat food … and both involve spoons! I'm sure you can picture it already! Anyway, she totally forgot which spoon was which … and found herself licking the wrong spoon!!! She didn't even realize what she was doing until our human brother said, in a very shocked voice, "Mom! You realize you are licking … cat food…?"

She discovered that our cat food was quite tasty and had a nice texture (we could have told her that!) but that it needed a bit more seasoning for her palate; however, she was happy to be able to say that she had taken her vitamins that day and that her coat would be quite shiny! Needless to say, we assured her that it was. It was so funny!

Some people say that cats don't laugh. I assure you that we do – even if you humans can't differentiate it from our other purrs - and we certainly laughed a lot that day! I think it's one of those days that none of us will ever forget … or allow her to forget, either! Every so often, I still hear my human brother reminding her about it as she prepares the rations for everyone;

However, this Christmas, Elaine sent Mom a special spoon which, hopefully, will prevent her from making that mistake again!

*   *   *   *   *   *   *

One night, after Jasper Poe had woken us all up yet again, we decided that it must be morning already and that it might be fun to run as fast as we could from one end of the house to another. Mom really wasn't at all happy. She got up and told us that we could practice for the Olympic trials when the sun was at least shining! I politely reminded her that I had gotten my name because I did my best work at the witching hour.

"In that case," she said, firmly, "I will have no problem in separating you all so that some people can actually sleep! Some of us have to go to work – or to school - in the morning!"

After that, I decided that I could use a nap myself and went to get in my basket. It worked! Once we do something cute, Mom forgets all about why she's not happy with us!

"Jasper, the forecast is good for tomorrow. If you stop singing and let us go to sleep, I will make sure that you get to see Columbia tomorrow," she said to my brother – at which he went all embarrassed and curled up to go to sleep too.

Before long, the entire house was at peace again – for a few hours, anyway!


However, it was not many weeks before he decided that he needed to entertain us with his greatest hits again! Add to that, Emmett Alexander's desperate need to practice NASCAR racing-style evasive moves at two o'clock, and it's not surprising that we were treated to the lecture about people and furry family members needing sleep time.

"OK, guys," she announced, "That's enough of the NAS-kitty practice, the Olympic trials and the auditions for American Idol

Reboot. You have all day to practice these; it doesn't need to be done at midnight. We all need our sleep! Your human brother and sister and I have to be up for school and work; and we will be no use to anyone if you all carry on like this!"

Needless to say, few of us were really listening! Night time shenanigans were far too much fun ... until Mom threatened that she might be too tired to remember to feed us! At that point, she most definitely had our attention.

## Ration Times

Ration times continued every morning and evening – and the food was always lovely. Mom had her own witchy recipes that ensured that most of our meds, vitamins and anything else that we needed were well and truly included and, although we were aware of it, the food was too yummy to avoid! She got us every time!

One morning, we had our own version of fight club at ration time. Arkham Darkham was being himself, as usual, and causing arguments with Biscotti Gotti, and none of us were particularly happy!

After that, Mom announced that we would have to spread out to eat! I had my designated seat under the table and my brothers and sisters had their separate places around the house. We all felt that this was cruel and unusual punishment, seeing how it was actually only two of us who seemed to have forgotten our manners. Emmett Alexander lodged his complaint for this grievous injustice in our human brother's room, which my human brother proceeded to sit in, causing even more of an uproar. As Mom said, that sort of thing always happens when they were due out of the door five minutes ago!

Finally, just as Mom was about to shoot out of the door with Jax, we were told that we could have some yard time today ... if we could be nice to each other. I decided that I would use the opportunity to case the perimeter, looking for weaknesses in our fenced in area. There were definitely times when I need to escape from this mad-house!

There were also times when I begin to think that Biscotti Gotti might actually be a genius! He literally followed Mom around the kitchen at ration times, ensuring that his bowl was filled first. Then, a bit later, I would watch him greet a stranger and I would have to take that back. Geniuses don't just go up to strangers and sniff their butts to say hello! I tried to explain to him that this behavior was quite off-putting to us cats, but the ability to listen really isn't one of his better skills.

I seriously had to wonder about some of my family members – BFFFs or not!

Of course, no family is complete without its arguments and discussions; and many of those came at ration time – like the time when Jasper Poe, normally so relaxed and chilled, took to hiding on top of the cupboard. This is what I heard.

> Mom: Jasper Poe, come down right now.
>
> Jasper: Nope, he touched me again.
>
> Arkham: No, I didn't.
>
> Mom: Jasper please come down.
>
> Jasper: Nope, not until you tell Arkham to stop hiding and waiting for people.
>
> Arkham: I don't!
>
> Jasper: Oh yes you do! You just did it!
>
> Mom: Oh, good grief, just come down so that I can feed you.
>
> Jasper: Only if you keep him out of the way.

Mom did just that, and Jasper Poe came down to eat; however, our feeding time was again delayed because Arkham Darkham can't keep his paws to himself. I really feel he should be in solitary confinement, particularly at ration times; Mom just says he's special. Yeah, I agree – specially challenging to the rest of us! Seriously??? That day, I was getting really determined about escaping.

I really mean it! We have to fight the establishment!


On another day, the conversation consisted of Mom telling Biscotti Gotti that he could not steal other people's treats. Of course, this went way over his head and he proceeded to steal treats from, of all people, Arkham Darkham! Talk about stupid! Naturally, this resulted in Arkham Darkham using his paws to take care of the matter, which led to Mom talking to all of us about manners and leaving others' things alone. However, I am fairly confident that neither one of them was listening, as this sort of behavior continued from time to time!

As I say, ration time could be somewhat frustrating!

# Long Car Rides

For some reason, Mom and my human family had to make a few long car rides from time to time. I never found out quite what was happening, but my canine siblings were most disgruntled! Neither Biscotti Gotti nor Garcia Maria Lopez could understand why they were not allowed to go on an eight-hour car ride.

I personally enjoyed those eight-hour car rides, even if none of us were actually allowed to go on them. It's amazing what you can shred when the humans are out for that amount of time! I tried to encourage the dogs and Emmett Alexander to help me but, alas, they do not take direction well.

I decided that, if these extended car rides continued, I might have to rethink my plans to escape. There's something rather fun about fighting the establishment!

## Yard Time

Yard time came, and yard time went.

There were days when no one got to go outside because it was too hot, (sarcastic eye rolling going on here!). Honestly, I would like to know who determines the temperature because our days are based on this number. Personally, I think I should be the one who decides, but no one listens to me.

At other times, it was too wet – and, at other times it was too cold! At times, it was hard to work it out from our climate-controlled home; however, rain was obvious!

Of course, when we were kept inside, one or other of my brothers would 'file a complaint' outside the litter box, somewhere or other – under the table, in Mom's favorite shoe, or her bath tub ... even on one of our brother's feet! Sometimes, these reached Mom; at other times, Biscotti Gotti would 'shred' them in his own, inimitable way! Me, I would just sit and stare at Mom in the hope that she would change her mind.

However, the way I really enjoyed starting my morning was outside with my mom and my other furry family members. It was really cool to know that I belonged and that I was loved.

One day, when it was particularly hot, Jasper Poe and I managed a full day of watching 'Bird T.V.' (i.e. looking out of the window and counting our avian visitors.) At the end, I was exhausted and found the perfect place to spend my evening. Mom was never getting this basket back, ever. It was like my indoor birdbath – mine, forever!

The following day, we finally got our much-awaited yard time. Unfortunately, because of a brother I won't name (Arkham Darkham being himself again!) we had to come in early. It was quite chaotic! The only ones not involved in mischief that day were me, of course – I was being an angel, as usual, supervising from my birdbath - and the one who usually ruins all our fun: Biscotti Gotti! He was inside eating his kabooble! Go us!

Of course, once again we had been working tirelessly on a hole as part of our escape plan, and it was becoming quite something, thanks mainly to Garcia Maria Lopez! (Did I say she was a great hole-digger?) It wasn't the first time that we had tried something like this but then, suddenly, the hole we had been working on tirelessly was filled in once again. To say we were peeved is to belittle the situation! In protest, we decided to use it as an outdoor poop receptacle.

After that, the dogs, whom I had thought were allies, seemed to abandon our cause for a while - but, then again, they are easily distracted – and there are lots of things in the garden to be distracted by. As for my fellow cats, well, least said, soonest mended!

Sadly, I had to reconcile myself to remaining in this enclosure with its flowers and shaded areas and chairs scattered around for sleeping. These conditions were quite deplorable, but my complaints went unheard. Fight the establishment!

On another day, when we had our yard time, Mom decided to take some pictures of us. I decided that her phone was dirty, so came over to clean it the best way that I know how! I'm not sure that she appreciated my help, as she then took it inside and wiped it down with a cloth. Sometimes, I'm not sure why I bother!

Of course, my favorite place in the entire garden was the birdbath. It was MINE! However, at times, I needed to remind some of the others of that fact, as this diary entry reflects!

Dear Diary

Guess who's back in the bird bath! I might have had to shoo someone else away, Emmett Alexander. I have tried repeatedly to tell the others this is mine, and there are plenty of other places for them. THE BIRD BATH IS MINE AND NO ONE ELSE'S!

P.S.
I might have had to pee on the bird bath. Unfortunately, this means nothing to either Emmett Alexander or Biscotti Gotti.

Fight the establishment with me! It's fun!

After a while, Mom and the other humans moved my bird bath over to a new site because, apparently, the humans were going shopping for another one after she was done at work. It seems that the birds actually wanted a real birdbath with water in it (go figure!) Clearly, that was not something that would appeal to me and so, because of this, MY birdbath was still MINE!

I sat there a lot over the next few weeks, contemplating life and ruling my kingdom in my own, inimitable way. As dictator of these people, my main job was supervision!

In the meantime, tunneling continued because we were determined. Garcia Maria Lopez and my least likely ally, Emmett Alexander, joined my cause. I wanted to celebrate but, at the same time, I was praying that Mom would not spot our progress, because I feared that she might start filling in our holes with cement – or something similar.

Unfortunately, that was when our human sister decided to break out the cat nip, resulting in the end of the useful work for another day. My brother, Emmett Alexander, started rolling around in it and then, to top it off, our human brother started blowing catnip bubbles!

How could we be expected to live in these conditions? As their dictator, I tried to stop this debauchery, but it was no use.

Unfortunately, that night, I overheard mom talking about a trip to the Lowes place, our local home improvement store. That can only mean more supplies to impede our progress.

Fight the establishment? We certainly kept on trying!


On another day, our plans for escape were derailed because the dogs got distracted by the flowers. They were having great fun picking up the plastic flowers and running around the garden with them. I decided to just sit back and watch the chaos as Mom chased them around, trying to get them back. I wonder if she actually realized that this had quickly become their favorite game?

It was highly frustrating, though, to a would-be prison escapee. No sooner would one of us start an impressive hole than Mom or Pops would fill it. It was like a never-ending battle.

This is how it typically went from one day to the next:

Day One

Dear Diary

Garcia Maria Lopez started a rather impressive hole; then Jasper Poe and Arkham Darkham continued it! All my fears that I was getting nowhere appear to be for nothing, because great progress was made today.

Just when I thought all hope of escape was lost, my hopes have been restored.

Day Two

Dear Diary

My mom has bought some hole filling materials that I am not
sure even the dogs can dig out. I shall find out what Quick
Crete is and destroy it!

Mom will not outsmart me.  Fight the establishment!

One day, after we'd had a few indoors days and the weather
forecast was finally beginning to look better, Mom announced
the fact that she was leaving work early, so we would be able to
play outside as long as we wanted!  I laughed my evil laugh to
myself because, by 'play' I meant plan my great escape!
Bruhahaha!  When would I finally succeed?

I kept on plotting and planning, but it was a thankless task!  My
brothers and sisters would start out well, and then it would all
go to pot as they got distracted.

Still, it kept me occupied!

Pops continued to look after us, dealing with wasps' nests after Biscotti Gotti had been stung; checking the garden and ensuring that we were always as safe as possible. I decided that I wasn't against seeing more of the world and we really are rather spoilt! Maybe it is worth staying; but whatever – the plotting and planning was still fun!

The weather still continued to cause us problems, preventing us from continuing with our plans and frustrating us in many ways but, nevertheless, we did our best to cause chaos and mayhem!

Dear Diary

Rain, rain go away!

It has rained all day, so no-one got to go outside; hence some cranky people. Biscotti Gotti is clearly feeling better after his visit to the Man with Pointy Things, because he chased everyone today. Arkham Darkham and Jasper Poe may have had a slight disagreement with their paws. Emmett Alexander may have found the secret stash of catnip. And I, of course, have been the absolute angel watching everything happen!!!

P.S. Tomorrow is supposed to be another rainy day so, once again, we will all be inside!

Sometimes, however, I have to say that it was just so cool to have these humans as my family. Although I was still plotting my escape, at times I just had to take a break from that to enjoy my family. After all, it was nice to remember the fact that I belonged somewhere!

## Bath Time

From time to time, Mom would announce that one or more of us of us needed a bath. Of course, sometimes, it had to be my turn - and I absolutely hated, loathed and detested baths.

One morning, Mom announced that I, along with Garcia Maria Lopez, would be getting said 'bath' that night before bedtime. What a threat! Enough to make any self-respecting cat want to hide! Honestly, how many dictators' moms forced them to be clean? None, I tell you, except for mine. I was totally fighting the establishment on this one. Baths are stupid!

I tried hiding under Mom's bed, but she lured me out, somehow with her normal witchery. There really is no escaping her when she is like that. Next thing I knew, I was in the bath and being washed. I sang the song of the people throughout, but Mom ignored me.

When she decided I was clean, she lifted me out and wrapped me in a towel. Next came the only bit that I like about bath night – the petting and cuddling! My human sister, Hayley took over and snuggled me until I was nearly dry; then I finished the process off with my tongue.

Dear diary

Apparently this would be dictator passed inspection along with Garcia Maria Lopez.

Tomorrow, I shall go out and dirty myself up again.

Seriously what kind of mother demands cleanliness? I hear her now telling my human brother he is next. We were also informed his room is a pig sty and, apparently, our mother is an authority on this. I tried to tell him to run, but he just sat there and kept petting me.

Once I am ruler of this kingdom baths are going to be outlawed, everyone shall be dirty. But, until then, I am due for my 20th nap of the day.

## Parties

Of course, no family is complete without celebrations!

The first real party I got to enjoy was Jasper Poe's Gotcha day – it was quite a celebration!

Mom made special bone-shaped dog treats and fish-shaped cat treats – but I have to say that both were delicious! There were also balloons and all sorts of things – we all had a whale of a time and were quite pooped by the end of it!

Best of all, as far as Jasper was concerned, was the fact that our neighbor's cat got to come to our house and hang out with Jasper for the evening. This is a picture of her sitting and trying to figure out why her humans brought her here!

Needless to say, Jasper was beside himself; he didn't even sing to her like he normally does.

Have I mentioned that, even though I kept trying to escape we had a pretty cool mom who is slightly off - but in a good way?

My human brother, Jax, had his birthday on 18th November, which resulted in another huge celebration! I was absolutely pooped after the party.

The human known as my brother wasn't the only one who got presents. We got a cat castle and a tube to share. The dogs got their favorite treats.

What I learned today is, humans are very weird. I still do not understand filling perfectly good boxes up with things. When I am in charge all boxes shall remain empty and waiting.

Jasper Poe constantly refused to let anyone else get in the castle. I waited patiently, aware that, eventually he would have to leave in order to get his rations; and when he did, I was determined to be in.

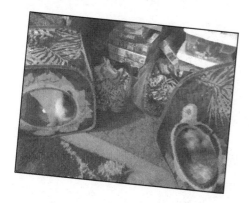

We also had a pawsome tube and two more hidey holes. The only problem was that Biscotti Gotti didn't get my memo about it being for CATS!

Oh well, Mom was always saying that I needed to share more.

## Our Cat Tree

We also have an amazing cat tree, which we all love to climb at times – but Emmett Alexander loves it the most ... particularly after Mom squirts it with catnip spray. At times like that, he puts on quite a performance. I kinda feel like I should leave him some money as payment for his performance ... except that someone would probably just eat it if I did!

## Collars – the bane of my life!

On the 1st September 2017, Mom bought me a brand-new collar and, guess what? I wore it for exactly one day and it disappeared – like magic! Mom couldn't understand it, but she said she was just glad our tag numbers were recorded at the vet.

All I can say is, don't blame me. That's black cats for you. We can make things disappear at the blink of an eye!

The following day, I had a brand-new blue collar with a bow tie. Mom said I could wear it on special occasions! Hmmm! I wasn't too sure about that!

I forget how many more I managed to 'lose' over the years ... probably enough to break a few banks – but Mom kept on buying them for me! No idea why! She even got me a bandanna at one point. Hmm!

## Introducing boxes!

Honestly, my family and their boxes! I have to say that we all love them, and we have been known to fight about them from time to time. At other times, we are happy to share.

I remember this conversation with my brother, Emmett Alexander, when he was trying to fit in this crazy, kitten-sized box.

> Me: Emmett, you will not fit in that box.
>
> Emmett: Oh, yes, I will.
>
> Me: No, you will not
>
> Emmett: Yes, I will.
>
> Me: This is getting ridiculous! Even though you have

no tail you still will not fit in there. It's far too small for you!

Emmett: See! I told you, Zero, I knew I would fit. I just had to turn in circles a few times and, magically, it happens!

Me: Whatever Emmett, believe what you need to. That box is yours if you want it! I'm not going to compete ... today!

A few weeks later, Mom found a rare moment to photograph our elusive princess. Harley Quinn when she found a box and couldn't resist getting in it.

Like I have said before she's our ninja; stealthy and only seen when she wants to be. She's a bit spoiled like the rest of us. Also, Harley Quinn is absolutely no help to my plight, she does what she wants and nothing else.

More about boxes later, as they are something that we all enjoy at times – even me!

## Biscotti Gotti

Let me explain Biscotti Gotti, my BFFF, more clearly. He may be disguised in cuteness, but don't be fooled! I have seen him decapitate a doll in less than a minute, and as for stuffed toys ... well ... they just don't stand a chance! A trail of stuffing can often be found leading to the carcass of some poor bear or bunny. In addition, he's a real hoarder. Everything from homework, utensils, coupons, rulers, pencils ... to an entire roll of toilet paper; if he can put it in his mouth, it goes to his special man cave/dog cave place.

Now Biscotti Gotti is supposedly still a puppy, so I have tried to cut him some slack, but seriously, he is slightly crazy ... and then you add in the cuteness and no one stands a chance! I am telling you he must have been a former high-ranking member of the mafia – although it's hard to imagine when you see him with my Nana, all wrapped up for winter!

I already mentioned the homework and how Biscotti Gotti likes to eat it, right? Here is Biscotti Gotti and our human brother, Jax, after said incident. As you can see my human brother thought it was hilarious, and Biscotti Gotti really had no defense. Seriously who leaves evidence in their mouth? If anyone doubted our human brother, mom said just tell them there is photographic evidence of why some of it looked the way it did.

I really had my doubts our mom would ever get it back!

One other thing about my brother, Biscotti Gotti, is that he just can't sleep without his pillow. From time to time, there could be a slight panic when said ugly pillow could not be found. (Bear in mind, 'slight' in Biscotti Gotti terms was always quite major in anyone else's!) Fortunately, it was usually quite quickly recovered allowing Biscotti Gotti to stop pacing and whining. In my opinion, Biscotti Gotti needed to learn to be more cat! We just sleep wherever we want, and I have never whined because I couldn't find my pillow or my woobie!

One evening in the middle of November, our human sister said that she kept hearing something going clunk. Now she said it was happening every couple of minutes. I was sitting in one of my usual perches, just watching. I could hear her talking to herself, wondering what the noise was. Finally, after several clunks she decided to see what was going on.

Well, apparently Mom forgot to put the little sack of dog treats away and Emmett Alexander took it upon himself to be the dispenser! Biscotti Gotti was quite happy about Emmett being in charge instead of our humans.

It was round about then that I noticed that Biscotti Gotti had started walking around with his tongue out! I couldn't decide if he was trying to be cool like me, or if he was trying to steal my trademark. Either way I planned to have a discussion with mom about this!

Another thing about my brother, Biscotti Gotti, is that he gets to make regular 'spa' visits for grooming sessions. He always got very excited about these. His groomer is a crazy lady who works with the Man with Pointy Things. She, however, doesn't have pointy things; she has shampoos and shiny, cutty things instead. She will groom anything - that's right, you heard me, I said anything! Cats, dogs – she even painted a horse's hooves once, so that it could look fancy for a show! However, she's considered so good at her job that it's almost impossible to get an appointment to see her unless you are a 'frequent flyer' like Biscotti Gotti.

Whenever she hands Biscotti Gotti back to Mom after he's all done, she will give him a kiss on his head. Crazy, I tell you! But then, I think Mom is kinda crazy too, because I have caught her giving my kisses to both dogs from time to time. Kisses? Gross! I am telling you, we dictators don't do kisses!

Now, whilst I did not enjoy baths and certainly would not have looked forwards to one of her spa treatments, Biscotti Gotti always started acting a fool as soon as he saw her – or even heard the words 'Spa day'. All I know is, every time he went, he would smell like something fancy for an hour after his return and then, inevitably, he would do something daft, and it would be as if he never had a spa day in the first place. I really don't know why Mom bothered!

Jasper Poe, the family member who's been here the longest, told me that, one time he heard Mom say Biscotti was getting a blue facial. Seriously, why does a dog of any kind need a facial of any kind? Sad thing is, apparently, he heard blueberry and got very excited, unfortunately! Jasper feared that he was going to be greatly disappointed, but no! Every time any member of our family goes to visit the Man with Pointy Things, Biscotti Gotti talks excitedly about blueberry facials!

# Escape-Gate

My ambition to escape continued with the start of many more tunnels but, to my horror, the first group to nearly succeed did not include me! No!

It was like this: Arkham Darkham and Emmett Alexander managed to make it out through the back door when Mom wasn't looking; they then got all the way to our neighbor's house, where they stopped to smell the flowers and were promptly apprehended and returned by said neighbor.

Honestly, if it had been me, would I have let myself get caught as easily as that, I ask you?

It's really is quite a problem getting away when your Mom is friends with several people who live on your road. Anyway, because of that, two of us were in time out, and all of us got to hear the lecture about how it's not safe to run away.

Clearly, escaping is going to take some extensive planning because everyone around here knows where we live.

# Back to the Man with Pointy Things

Because of my mouth and snot problems, I still had to make regular visits back to the Man with Pointy Things. In early September, after a few of those visits, I was told I was 'good for now' by said man, who is now some kind of authority about me, and this was great news!

Some of you on Cat House asked the question, "What was wrong with his mouth?" Well, it seems I was born with my jaws not aligning right, which causes me to drool sometimes, and my tongue constantly sticks out. Apparently, the first time I visited the Man with Pointy Things, I must have been a real mess because, every time he saw me after that, he went on and on about how good I looked. My humans say I was always adorable but, when I first came to them, I was missing fur and very malnourished - which is why I had to continue to take vitamins all the time I lived with them. As a result, within a few months, I was healthy and very shiny, albeit with some occasional drool on my chin.

Of course, every time I come back from visiting the Man with Pointy things, I always shared my tasty treats with everyone (even the dogs) because that's how I roll. Besides, Biscotti Gotti would always be waiting for me to come home, which was rather nice. You see, we had this little seat by the window where we could sit and look out. Every time Mom had to take me to see the Man with Pointy Things, Biscotti Gotti would sit there and wait, patiently, for me to come home. As soon as Mom walked into the house, carrying me in my special carrier, Biscotti Gotti would jump up and down, yapping to greet me; his little tail wagging like crazy. It was like I had me very own 'Welcome home' party. Sometimes, he would even bring me part of a toy or a headless doll as a 'welcome home' present – but I wasn't always well enough to play with it. I think he understood, because he's very forgiving like that. Sometimes, he's a really cool best friend to have!

By the end of October, Mom had extracted the pet carrier again. Once again, it was lined with fluffy soft things; but that does not change the destination. My woobie (my special blanket) was in there, so I knew it was for me!

Lo and behold, off I went for another trip to visit the Man with Pointy Things.

It turned out that I had a little sinus infection which was causing me to drool more than usual. According to the Man with Pointy Things, a few added vitamins along with the shot I got in the thigh and some antibiotics should take care of it. But, just to be sure, he told Mom that he wanted to pet me again in a week. (I was fairly sure that he just said 'pet me' so I would come back) however, I did receive an entire snack bag of Halloween treats for my discomfort – which wasn't too bad! The other members of the furry family were certainly happy to see them, and even Edward Enigma got a few as a special treat!

What I want to know is this: why do the Man with Pointy Things and Mom always say they are so sorry, and yet I still get a shot? I don't think they are sorry at all. I wonder if any of my other cat comrades encounter this problem?

As usual, Biscotti Gotti was waiting for me when I got home, sitting on the seat by the window. He greeted me with a rubber chicken that he had started to annihilate – but I really didn't feel up to helping him. All I wanted was the therapeutic mattress on Mom's bed. Before long, Garcia Maria Lopez joined me, and she did not leave my side until I started to feel more like myself. While she is not a very focused worker, she has always been a very loyal friend.

When we are outside, she is our protector along with Biscotti Gotti. When we are not feeling well, she is our nap buddy.

Don't tell the others, but Garcia Maria Lopez is my new best friend!

After a couple of days of the icky medicine and vitamins, my drooling started to improve, and I started to feel more like myself. However, when I went back to the Man with Pointy Things on the following Monday, there was still a little snot, so he stuck me again with one of his nasty pointy things, which he followed quickly up with a scratch to my ears.

He told me that I had to return on Friday in order for him to shine a light in my face, listen to my chest area and to pet me a bit more because I was so adorable! Hmm! I may be a cat, but black cats are not so easily fooled! Something mysterious was definitely afoot here! Mom kept telling me that it was necessary, but I wasn't so sure.

Still, I did receive some lovely treats and, because our family is so big, and the Man with Pointy Things knows us so well, he sent extras for everyone. He even told me that, if I was really good, there might be a surprise for me on Friday. OK- but was that another cunning way of encouraging me to come back, I wondered.

When Friday came, I was put back in my carrier, along with my woobie, and was taken back again, where I was finally given the all clear. Apparently, after shining a light in my eyes, swabbing my mouth and scratching my ears again, the Man was able to determine this. I reckon he must be some kind of magician to be able to work all this out so easily!

After all of this, I was picked up by this same man, petted and scratched behind my ears a lot more; which, I have to say, I very much enjoyed (even if I tried to pretend that I didn't).

Needless to say, we have a pretty cool vet and, because he knows us so well, the Man with Pointy Things gave Mom lots of treats to share with everyone – including a bonus stash especially for me. Even Mom got a sucker this time (peanut-butter flavored, of course. I told you he knows us well!).

## Family Photos

At some stage, the decision was made that we were supposed to try and take a family picture for some strange reason. As I was well aware, this was probably going to be near to impossible because certain family members can't be still. Plus, has anyone ever actually tried to line up two dogs, five cats and three humans?

Anyway, after several failed attempts, all the humans gave up –
and who blamed them?  Biscotti Gotti and Garcia Maria Lopez
were more interested in a shoe; Harley Quinn was just not
having it; and Arkham Darkham ran and hid. So, this is what they
got: me and two of my brothers, Jasper Poe and Emmett
Alexander.

What you can't see is I literally fell asleep while all this was
going on.  Really, these people think we can help with
organization? Have they not met us?  Perhaps if there was some
kind of medication for some of us; but even then, that's not a
guarantee

# Hiding from Mom

From time to time, one or other of us would decide that it would be fun to hide from Mom. Harley Quinn was always the best at this – hence her nickname of The Ninja, but I was prepared to give it a go too, and I was getting better at it! After all, have you ever just laid there, listening as a woman walking around calling every name you might answer to?

One day, I decided to try a different place - the laundry room! It seemed like a great place for a nap.

Unfortunately, when she finally found me, Mom was more than a little upset and I had to endure a lecture about not hiding - especially in the laundry room. It was then quarantined off from me. Moms can be real party poopers at times!

## Dog-gate

Unfortunately, the people who live down the road from us suddenly acquired a rather large dog and I mean *large!*) The problem that our Mom had to work on was this: they just let their dog run free! Mom said it scared her because this dog could easily grab one of us and hurt us, so we were stuck inside until a solution could be found.

When I expressed our worries, Mom assured me that she would find a solution but, in the meantime, the natives were restless. As usual, 'complaints' were filed in various places outside the litter tray ... and, equally as usual, some were eaten ... however, in the meantime, we all had to wait.

We were lucky! Three days later, we all got a few minutes outside before Mom had to leave for work. We were assured that, when she was done at work, we would get to play outside again. The dog from down the road had now been kept properly restrained and Mom said it looked like they may finally be building a fence.

That evening, our lovely Pops came over to walk the property line and make sure there were no problems. He also checked our fenced area to make sure it was still all good. I have to say it – we really are lucky to have these amazing humans who make sure we are always safe and accounted for here – and, when I see a big dog like that, I feel a little less eager to escape. It really was quite frighteningly BIG!

# Shoe-Gate

Due to the fact a pair of shoes appeared to have been eaten one day in October, whilst the humans were away, Biscotti Gotti and Garcia Maria Lopez had to go to our Nana and Pops' house. I think this was supposed to be a punishment but, when the lady known as Nana gives you treats and kisses, it sort of defeats the purpose.

I tried to tell them eating shoes was inappropriate behavior, do they listen? Nope! So that day, we cats had the house to ourselves! Bruhahaha!

However, here is the picture our Nana sent to our Mom later in the day. As you can see, they were enduring a great and terrible punishment! Snuggling with Pops is torture (not!) And to be covered in blankets, someone should file a complaint, absolutely horrendous!

Seriously, someone needs to rethink punishments in this house!

## Coping with Winter Weather

Winter in Oklahoma means really cold weather. It can settle in from the end of October onwards, and so there is a lot of cuddling and snuggling from then onwards.

We each find our own special places to curl up, and that is where we stay – even (or especially) if it is inconvenient to the humans! You know how I like to fight the establishment! Bruhahaha!

Dear Diary

Today, Mom thought she would organize things and tidy the house. She also thought she could use the table. As you can see, she was wrong. I politely declined her request to move my basket to a new spot!

P.S. Unfortunately it is very cold here and very windy, so I have been told we are inside for the time being. I shall rule from my basket the next few days.

Emmett Alexander and Jasper Poe, clearly best friends for life, love to curl up on their blankets together rather than work! Where one is, you will usually find the other.

When it got really cold, Mom would break out the puppy pads for the dogs, so that they didn't have to go out either. Obviously, we (the cats) had our litter trays, so we were fine ... or at least we should have been!   However, here is the conversation Mom had with Emmett Alexander on one particularly cold morning.

Mom: Emmett, what are you doing?

Emmett: I have absolutely no idea what you are talking about.

Mom: Really, Emmett, because it looks like you are peeing on the puppy pads.

Emmett: Why would you think that?

Mom: Maybe because I saw you, and now you are trying to cover it up by scratching the pee pad.

Emmett: No, you must be seeing things. I was helping Biscotti Gotti cover his pee up because, well, that's just good manners.

Mom: Whatever, Emmett!

Alas, we were scheduled for cold weather for the next couple of days, so I was well aware that Mom and Emmett were likely to have this conversation a few more times in the near future.

## Halloween

Mom and I loved Halloween ... and handing out candy. Every time the trick-or-treaters called, she had to answer the door whilst holding on to me, because I always had to know exactly what was going on. Plus, I just liked being petted by all the little trick or treaters before they got their candy!

Nevertheless, Mom and I were always a little nervous about the fate of black cats at this time of year, as they can experience a few problems and some real nastiness if they're outside, so she always looked after me especially carefully around Halloween and urged other people with house panthers like me to do the same.

## Frustrations and Perturbations

Early in November, I reached the stage where I was getting more perturbed and frustrated than ever. (This picture shows my perturbed face!) Absolutely no work was happening, for a wide range of reasons.

First was Biscotti Gotti's tendency to eat anything and everything that he saw. If I had to listen to one more lecture on trash and how we do not eat it, I knew that I would not be responsible for my actions! Biscotti Gotti, for some reason, seemed to enjoy these talks as he just sat there, trying to imitate me with his tongue out, and wagging his tail. In the meantime, did we get any work done? The answer was a resounding no.

Next came the catnip saga.

Arkham Darkham, thought it would be a good idea to indulge, which resulted in him making an enormous mess in the middle of the floor. Of course, our catnip addict, Emmett Alexander, then had to roll around in it and getting it all in his fur, which led to Garcia Maria Lopez thinking he needed a bath.  This is all ended with Emmett Alexander using his paws to let Garcia know that he really needed no help with cleaning.

Needless to say, very little work was done that evening.  How can I be a successful dictator when the people I am dictating refuse to listen? I have never in my life seen people who are so easily distracted.

And I could see that it wasn't going to get any better very quickly!  The next day, for reasons best known to himself, Emmett seemed to be upset about something because he filed a complaint on Mom's lovely shoes, so he was in trouble again. On top of that, Arkham Darkham couldn't seem to go more than five minutes without someone yelling his name; and don't get me started on the others!

Harley Quinn was, in many ways, the only slightly reliable member of the family, but she was always elusive and only spoke to me on occasions. Jasper Poe just sat back and took everything in; which I believed could be a great resource to me in the future and Garcia Maria Lopez either wagged her tail or slept.

I would say they were like monkeys; but monkeys I would at least be able to train!

Finally, in frustration, I told Biscotti Gotti to stay out of the trash because none of us wanted another lecture on how we were not homeless and didn't need to eat from the garbage; also, because none of us wanted the lecture about having to go see the Man with Pointy Things because of bugs!

Was it really too much to ask? Clearly so as, only the next day, he was back in it again!

* * * * * *

In the meantime, Mom told me that thousands of people were reading my diary and commenting on it. This led to me telling Mom, "Hey, why not get these people to help others like me!"

Needless to say, she thought that it was a brilliant idea, so she started by encouraging people to help where they could, with posts like this:

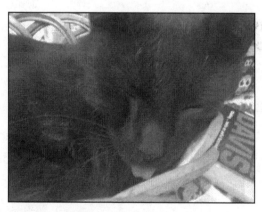

Zero says night-night.

From being so ornery, sometimes I catch him being so sweet, like now.

Having said that I want to encourage anyone who is thinking about rescuing, please do it. There are so many Zeros out there that have just been cast aside because they need a little more love and time. Don't be afraid to adopt an older cat, or one like Zero that some would say is defective because, I assure you, Zero is just like all our other cats. He loves to play, cuddle, torment the others, and just be a spoiled kitty.

Remember, whenever you adopt, you are actually saving three: the one you take home has provided a space for another animal and, also, the adoption fee helps to feed another.

Incredibly, people started donating their time and money to help. Many people started looking into fostering and into educating people about this. It was a start, but I knew that there were so many more that needed help.

In the meantime, my life was more than I could ever have imagined. I had a family: a Mom, brothers and sisters (both human and furry) and my revolution had begun! I was Zero, but I was far from being nothing ... I was Zero Dark Thirty, and I was home!

# Chapter 7 – Thanksgiving and Christmas Mischief.

Winter came, and with it the fun of Thanksgiving, followed swiftly by Christmas with its boxes (everyone's favorite thing) and, also, the saga of the Christmas Village, which kept a great many people entertained throughout the Christmas period.

## Thanksgiving

One day, towards the end of November, I heard the humans discussing Thanksgiving which, I soon learnt, meant turkey, and lots of pumpkin things. I for one was getting very excited. Many people don't know this, but pumpkin (without any of the added spices that humans like) is a very tasty addition to a cat's diet – and it's really good for us too.

Mom said that Thanksgiving was a time to be grateful, so I told her that I was grateful that Jasper Poe had not sung the song of our people in a few days. She laughed at this and said that she, too, was thankful for this small mercy. Next, I whispered that, maybe, if I appear extra thankful, we would be able to skip the vitamins for one day! This one, she wasn't so sure about.

Finally, the big day arrived. Turkey was had (thank you Nana! What a treat this was ... for us all!) The Christmas tree survived another day, and Mom put up some amazing lights that went on and off. We sat for hours, trying to figure out what was going on! Eventually, we all gave up and went for naps!

Here is the message that Mom and I posted on Cathouse for Thanksgiving.

23rd November 2017

Dear diary

My family and I want to wish everyone a very happy Thanksgiving. Thank you all for letting us share a tiny part of your day with our wackiness.

To all our rescuers and adopters out there, I know I speak for every one of us who have been saved by saying thank you.

Thank you, also, to all the shelters who offer forgotten animals a second chance.

Thank you to everyone who gives their time and volunteers, like my humans; thank you for the donations you make.

To all my comrades; I have not given up on escaping, but heat on demand is very nice, and humans who cuddle and pet you whenever you walk by is pretty great - still I shall have my day!

So happy turkey day to you all.

Zero

# The Great Duck Caper

Every year, Mom and my human brother and sister set up an amazing Christmas Village close to the Christmas tree. There are houses, people, animals, transport ... anything that you could expect in a village!

Unfortunately, as you know, our house is a bit of a zoo. You would think that Mom and my human siblings would have realized by now that a Christmas village in our zoo was maybe not the brightest of ideas ... but... well, you know my family by now. What's more, each year something new was added. And this year was no exception.

On the 20<sup>th</sup> November, the village arrived and was set up because we had to be ready by Thanksgiving. The newest characters in 2017 were a family of ducks ... and they kept everyone entertained for weeks – not just in the house; but all over the world!

Unfortunately, it only took a few hours before the first casualty was announced - when Jasper Poe decided to re-enact a scene from Godzilla and a poor, unsuspecting villager was crushed. (Actually, it was all quite funny watching it from my place on the back of a chair!)

A couple of days later, disaster struck for real, when the ducks went missing. Rewards of treats were offered to anyone who knew their whereabouts, but they were still not returned.

We all had our suspicions as to who to blame. I gave Mom 3 guesses and told her that the first two didn't count ... but still the ducks weren't found.

After a couple of days, I actually suggested the names of two culprits, (not just Biscotti Gotti, but also Arkham Darkham), but the ducks were nowhere to be seen. We all searched everywhere – particularly in Biscotti Gotti's man-cave/dog-cave place, and the ducks were mentioned in nearly every post that Mom and I wrote. It became known as the Great Duck Caper; and people from all over the world checked in daily to see if they had been found. Every day, we had to post the sad news that they were still missing – running free somewhere in the house, we hoped! Our online friends suggested loads of great places to look, and Mom tried them all – but there was no joy. At one point, I even heard her declare that she never thought that she would be looking for the ducks in the litter box but, fortunately for them (and her!) no ducks were uncovered there.

A few days later, it got worse when one of the villagers disappeared. Mom threatened to interrogate a certain little dog later – and I reminded her that I had been telling her just this – two words: Biscotti Gotti! Another search of his dog-cave place unearthed part of a bird (fake) belonging to my human sister; several coupons; a spoon; and ... yet more of my human brother's homework! Mind you, it wasn't the first time, so maybe his teachers were expecting his 'the dog ate my homework ... again' as an excuse by now. All I can say is this: try keeping anything safe with our resident Hitman in the house!

Before long, the villager was found, but not the ducks. Personally, I thought they might have been buried during one of Biscotti Gotti's trips to the restroom in the garden. It was all a huge mystery, however, and great fun was had by all as more and more potential hiding places were suggested by online friends. Myself, I reckoned that Mom should just go shopping for replacements!

Lo and behold, after a week or so, she went out and bought more little people and more trees. Honestly, this is why I should have been in charge. I would have made better life choices in regard to decorating!

> Dear Diary
> Today, Mom was talking to Biscotti Gotti about said missing ducks, and as usual he just sat there looking cute, so she totally forgot what she was doing.
> Instead of jail, she patted his head and said, "Who's a good boy?" and then gave him one of his special Doggy- Christmas Cookies!

She's not very good at interrogating. He's put those ducks somewhere only he will ever know.

## Christmas Trees

Naturally, we didn't just have one tree to destroy.! There were always several in our house – just to add to the fun.

The main tree made it almost two whole days before Emmett Alexander and Arkham Darkham decided that it needed to be climbed. As a result, the top became vented. Mom declared that it was going to stay that way because it gave it character! Our resident princess just sat back and watched the entire show. Quite honestly, Harley Quinn could not be bothered with such nonsense; plus, she found Emmett Alexander quite vexing at times.

Sadly, on one or two occasions, 'complaints' were filed under said tree, which our princess found even more vexing; as it was her favorite place to sit! I knew that I would have to talk to my brothers about appropriate places to file their 'complaints' – after all, it's every brother's job to look after their sisters!

Needless to say, Harley Quinn soon found another favorite spot – in amongst the fake poinsettias that Mom arranged. I didn't see them lasting too long, either; however, it took a while for Mom to find her there! As I say, 'Where in the world is Harley Quinn' is not a game that she is very good at yet!

Soon after this, Mom went out to buy us our very own trees. She told us she couldn't care less if we destroyed them, as long as we left the main tree alone. What a great challenge! I could think of some people who would be happy to have a go at it – but would they be willing to forego the real tree?

One of these trees was a pink, sparkly one, which Arkham Darkham decided was his worst enemy and so I was certain that it would meet its demise well before Christmas ... and it did!

Arkham Darkham also insisted that his help was needed with the last stages of the decorations – the stockings and the lights. The only problem is that, realistically, the only time you need Arkham Darkham's help is if you are doing demolition.

But Arkham Darkham was not the only one to offer his help. I was there too! I thought she might need a hand with the final touches. So many pretty, twinkling lights that needed to be put up, and who better to assist than me?

Here is a picture of the hole that appeared in our main tree. It was perfect for sitting or taking a nap – which, I think, everyone except the dogs tried. Our seven-foot tree suddenly started to lean like the Leaning Tower of Pisa.

Of course, Mom had alternative ideas for the use of the hole. She decided that it was perfect for holding some of the smaller gifts. However, before very long, Emmett Alexander and Jasper Poe decided that she had created a new game especially for them. She would put the parcels in there, and they would swat them straight out again! All you could hear was "Emmett Alexander, Jasper Poe – quit knocking things out!" This was followed by our Mom scratching them behind the ears and telling them what pretty boys there were! Seriously? Someone should speak to her about punishment – I really don't think she knows how!

## More About Boxes

One of the frustrating things about Thanksgiving and Christmas is the way that humans just don't know how to use boxes. I mean, honestly! Surely, they should be used for their real purpose from the start – and us cats certainly know what that real purpose is.

I, personally, was quite fond of the box with all the unused Christmas decorations; it was perfect for my naps.

Then there's the game that my human brother and sister call 'Cat Physics'. Arkham Darkham and Emmett Alexander are particularly good at this one. To solve the problem, they go through three steps.

1)  First, walk around your chosen box three times.

2)  Next, step in and out of said box three times

3) Finally, get into the box and figure out whatever contortionist moves you need to use in order to fit in the box.

There you are!  Cat Physics 101!

One day, I overheard this funny conversation between Mom and the master of mayhem himself after a particularly impressive display of cat physics.

Arkham Darkham: See!  I told you I would fit!

Mom: I didn't say that you wouldn't.  I just said I wasn't sure you would; there is absolutely no reason for the stink eye or attitude.

Arkham Darkham: Well excuse me for being offended that you were insinuating that I might be too big. Woman, I tell you, in a former life I was a contortionist!

Mom: Whatever, Arkham.  Enjoy your box!

Arkham Darkham isn't the only one to ensure that boxes are used for their real purpose. We have all been known to occupy any box that we find lying around – even when Mom might actually want it for something else!

Emmett: What do you mean, you need this box? I just got in it!

Mom: I need it to wrap some of the Christmas presents, Emmett. I need you to be a good boy and get out, please

Emmett: No!

Mom: Not even for treats?

Emmett: Well, maybe - if you insist. Just let me sit here a bit longer!

Mom: Whatever, Emmett. As long as I get it back soon to wrap the presents in it!

Emmet: That depends on what you mean by soon!

Mom: The sooner it is, the more treats you will get!

It's not surprising that Emmett got out quite quickly after that, leaving Mom to use the box for totally the wrong purposes - I am clearly going to have to teach her about the proper use of boxes before next Christmas comes around. Seriously, why waste all that time filling them up just to empty them, when you could just make cat caves out of them to begin with?

## Supervising Ourselves.

One day, early in December, Mom told us that we would be unsupervised on the following day because, even if it killed her, she was going to finish the Christmas shopping.

Needless to say, the next day, I put myself in charge; after all, I am a dictator! First order of business was a nap, followed by an after-nap nap. I also decided to take time to do some self-grooming because, unlike some people (Biscotti Gotti!) it was something that I could handle myself.

I thought I could then follow that up with another nap – as long as my furry brothers and sisters behaved – which, fortunately, they managed for once! It seemed as though napping was high on all our priority lists that day – not least because we knew it would give us more energy for when the humans got back, exhausted! (Bruhahaha!)

When Mom and my human family got back, it turned out that one of the places they had visited was Petco (yippee!) and they had brought back a wide variety of treats for us. Exciting! Naturally, we had to investigate.

Now, seriously, all Emmett Alexander's job was, was to be the lookout but, apparently, he thought Garcia Maria Lopez and I needed him to help. This resulted in our humans hearing the rustling of paper, which caused Mom to come in and confiscate the treats that, in her fatigue, she had forgotten to put away. She scratched our ears as she stored said treats in their basket.

"Good try, guys, but all these have to wait until Christmas to be shared out!" she told us.

I couldn't believe it. Another failure! Seriously, my help here is so unreliable. What can I do? The only thing that they have mastered is the 'What are you talking about?' look.

Good help is so very hard to find. How am I going to escape if they can't even smuggle illicit pet treats at Christmas time?

Another clear failure. I will persevere!

## Sickness All Around

For once, I kept well over the Christmas period, but two of our number had to make trips to the Man with Pointy Things.

The first of these was my human brother, who developed bronchitis. He felt really rough, but we all gathered round to look after him because we all care about one another here.

Mom here

I wanted to share a little about this picture I took this morning.

My son has been really sick. He has bronchitis and has just been not well. Anyone who tells me animals don't feel, this picture speaks volumes.

Garcia Maria Lopez has literally stood guard by my son making sure he is alright. And Biscotti Gotti and Arkham Darkham have taken to following him around and either sitting or lying by him.

My heart was so full this morning because I know my son feels terrible, but he has these crazy animals that literally are watching over him.

As a lot of you know, we have a crazy family, but somehow humans and animals have made these incredible bonds, and all of us take care of each other.

Misty

Hey, what can I say? That's how we roll as a family!

He continued to feel very ill, so I insisted on Mom moving my box into my human brother's room because I didn't think I could rely on these humans to give him the proper care. Sometimes I slept on his bed, and sometimes I slept in the box because I really didn't want him to have to visit the Man with Pointy

Things; I knew, from first-hand experience, that was where he would go if he didn't quit with the snot. Mind you, perhaps he would bring us back some yummy treats to share ... and the pets and snuggles aren't so bad! But then, Mom told me that my brother sees a different Man with Pointy Things. I just hoped that, at least, he would get treats and ear-rubs there!

Then, one night, my bed was invaded! You see, I normally share Mom's bed because I love her therapeutic mattress but, on this particular occasion, Mom and I had to sleep on the couch because there was no room for anyone else in our bed. I supposed that was OK really, because my human brother was not feeling good. He still had some snot, and we all knew what that meant. Several of my brothers and sisters continued to look after him, because that's how we roll in this house.

The only problem, in my opinion, was that Jasper's Christmas present came early. His girlfriend came to stay with us whilst her human was travelling for the holidays. Oh, happy days! She made herself right at home, lounging on the pillow as if she owned the place!

After a few days, my human brother's meds started working; he began to feel somewhat better and Mom decided that he was ready to go back to school. At this point, Emmett Alexander and Jasper Poe decided to stage a rebellion that was not under my direction. They thought that, by blocking our human brother from his bag, they would be able to prevent him and Mom from leaving the house. Sadly, their attempt was not successful.

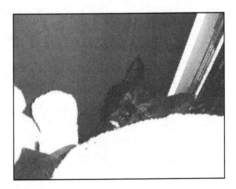

I was still taking my vitamins every day and wasn't too keen! This was the face that Mom got from me at times when she would ask me if I was ready to get my vitamins. No, I was not ready to get my vitamins – I would never be ready to get my vitamins. I didn't care if they did make my fur shiny, or they did make me healthy. I felt that she should ask the Man with Pointy Things about this! It all seemed sketchy to me, but, even as a would-be dictator, I had to go along with her!

The next member of the family to fall ill was my brother from another mother, Biscotti Gotti. Apparently, dogs like him also get snotty noses, so he went to the Man with Pointy Things. Fortunately, he loves driving in the car with Mom, so all he heard was "Let's go!" and he was off! (With hindsight, I bet he thought he was going for a spa day!) Looking at her face, I think Mom quite enjoys driving with him too!

All I could think as I saw them leave was, I hoped he would bring some of those tasty Christmas treats back with him!

Later, when he returned from his exile, we learnt that Mom needs to make sure he is not out too long when it's very cold because dogs like him tend to get colds, causing them to have a snotty nose. Medicine was given and had to be taken. Fortunately, as I know I have said before, Biscotti Gotti will eat anything, so giving him medicine is an easy task for Mom!

I tried to give him the same advice I gave my human brother: quit with the snot; but does he listen?

## The Twelve Days of Christmas – My Version

My human family kept playing this strange song about the 12 days of Christmas, where someone kept getting all sorts of strange gifts. If it were me, I wouldn't want half those things – I mean, what use are 5 gold rings to a cat? And so, after listening to it a few times, I decided to write my own Kitty version for Jasper Poe's next recital. Here's the last verse.

On the 12th day of Christmas, my humans gave to me:
- 12 kitty blocks,
- 11 red dots dancing,
- 10 pieces of string,
- 9 cat-nip mice,
- 8 pillows to lay on,
- 7 cardboard boxes,
- 6 cans of tuna,

- 5 missing ducks,

- 4 runaway villagers,

- 3 shiny ornaments,

- 2 pieces of wrapping paper,

- 1 bell to bat around.

I can only keep my paws crossed and hope! After all, who needs a partridge in a pear tree?

## Our Christmas Message

Somewhere, I heard that the Queen of England broadcasts a Christmas Message to her people every year, so I decided I would help Mom to post one to our people from us. We couldn't make it a national broadcast, but we could at least publish it on Cat House!

24th December 2017

Our entire family want to take a moment to wish everyone a Merry Christmas and to thank all of you for letting us share a little bit of our chaos.

Thank you to each and every one who has rescued, sheltered or donated time or money to help a furry friend. We love reading all your stories and seeing all the pictures.

I hope that all the animals who are waiting for your furever homes get them soon; and to all of you who have given a furever home to a previously unwanted animal, I hope you have a cat-tastic Christmas!

As of right now, we are all just chilling, waiting for our favorite people to come over (Nana and Pops) because, as many of you know, they always come bearing gifts for us all!

So again, we hope everyone, human and animals alike have a very Merry Christmas.

Zero ... and Mom.

# Chapter 8 – From Winter into Spring

Once Christmas was over and we moved into the new year, I managed to pick up a few sniffles and, over the next six months, had to make several trips to the Man with Pointy Things. Naturally, these resulted in me having to take lots of meds – most of which Mom, with her witchery, managed to sneak into my food. From time to time, I tried to avoid her – but she's far too sneaky and she caught me every time.

With hindsight, I guess she was doing it for the best – but, at the time, it was more than just a bit frustrating.

# Parties!

Emmett Alexander's birthday is at the end of December and, as you know, his favorite thing is boxes.

Ok, who am I kidding?  All of us love boxes – even our human brother; so, we basically had a day of playing in boxes because it was way too cold to be outside!

Garcia Maria Lopez had her birthday in January too.  We had amazing dog cookies (which we all like!) and delicious cat treats – including catnip of every variety.  By the end of the day, we were all pooped once again.


Towards the middle of February, we found that the humans kept saying 'Happy Birthday' to Mom so we realized that she had a special day too, which was a lovely surprise. I'm pleased to say that she had a fantastic day.  Instead of presents, she asked people to donate to one of their local shelters, which many people did, making Mom very happy!  All I know is that Emmett Alexander saw the balloons and went straight into hiding – as usual!  He's really not too keen on them.

In other news, one of our members (Biscotti Gotti) might have managed to snag a piece of cake during Mom's birthday and taken it to his man-cave/dog-cave place!

Afterwards, Biscotti Gotti was all partied out. Fortunately, most of the cake was stashed in said dog-cave, along with some caramel wrappers, an unopened can of cat food, a medicine cup, and a pencil (but still no ducks). Personally, I think he is one wrapper away from being on that show 'Hoarders', but I'd still like to know what he did with those poor ducks at Christmas!

Days like that were incredible and amazing fun and made me less inclined to want to escape. Our family really know how to celebrate together. I've heard it said that families that play together, stay together. That's us!

## Fun and Games

Naturally, during the colder months of the year, we were often denied yard time because the prison guards were afraid that it might cause us to get sniffles. As a result of this, we had to find ways to entertain ourselves

In early January, someone (Biscotti Gotti) may have gotten into the baby powder. That someone may have convinced others to roll in it (Garcia Maria Lopez). They may both have then proceeded to spread it around the bathroom, resulting in an episode that was up there with the toilet paper incident in November, when the humans had been on those long car journeys!

On another day, the humans in the family had been shopping and decided that it would be a 'good idea' to buy stuffed toilet paper for the canines in the family. The problem, as far as I was concerned, was that it crinkled, it squeaked, and it was highly annoying.

I, for one, was not particularly amused. They can keep their squeaky toilet paper. The real stuff is much more fun! Bruhahaha!

*   *   *   *   *

I know I've said it before, but Harley Quinn can be such a princess at times; however, some of us still try to impress her on and off. This is what it looks like when Emmett Alexander tries. Needless to say, she was not impressed and even tried to swipe at him with her paw a couple of times. She really is not easily impressed by much.

Then there was the day when Arkham Darkham decided to be a 'business kitty'! (Actually, he was trying to hide after having an argument with Garcia Maria Lopez, which Mom proceeded to tell everyone was 'inappropriate'.) His look of "I have absolutely no idea what you are talking about" and his choice of hiding place got Mom, and she totally forgot why he was supposed to be in time out. Again, I know I've said it before, but our Mom needs to learn about punishment!

## Protests

I was frustrated by the fact that we didn't get much yard time when the weather was so variable. I couldn't occupy the birdbath, and so I needed to find another place that would be MINE!

First of all, I decided to try occupying the sink, so that my humans had to work round me, and it worked ... at least, to a certain extent, it did! It was almost like having my very own indoor birdbath! There were just two problems. The first one was that it only slowed the humans down a little bit; the other one – and perhaps the more problematic of the two - was caused by my human brother, who tended to leave toothpaste in the sink after he had brushed his teeth. As you know, unlike my canine brother Biscotti Gotti, I detest baths, and I was quite upset to discover that a bath was the preferred method for removing toothpaste from my fur.

Sinks are cool, but baths are yucky!

Next, I moved onto occupying the bed – which was particularly effective at night (bruhahaha!). It seemed to cause slight confusion for the humans, as they oohed and ahhed, saying things like "How cute he is!" and "I hate to move him, but ..."

However, within a week or so, I was back to occupying the sink. My thought was "If I do it often enough, it will be just like my birdbath. It will be MINE!"
It seemed to work, so I will continue! At least, I will continue as long as my human brother keeps his toothpaste to himself and the weather keeps me out of my birdbath!


I don't know what Arkham Darkham's complaint was, though, and will have to speak to him later about lodging it right in the middle of the dining room floor. Definitely not acceptable behavior! I keep telling him that we have litter trays for a reason, but will he listen?

# Illness

### January

After a really healthy period over November and December, I had to make an unplanned trip to the Man with Pointy Things at the beginning of January. I was really congested and was not feeling at all well.

It turned out that I had a cold, which was causing all my nasty snot problems and was just making me feel icky. The Man with Pointy Things assured us, after some meds, I would soon be back to ruling as the dictator I had always been.

Mom was also educated on the visit. It turns out that, just like humans can get dried out nasal passages, so can animals. Immediately, Mom started running a cool mist humidifier to help me and my furry brothers and sisters because, unfortunately, it was still cold here and the heater was running all the time.

Mom posted the fact that I was feeling under the weather on the Cat House on the Kings Facebook page (if you haven't discovered it yet, have a look,) and I received lots of great vibes through your posts, all urging me to feel better. I was really appreciative of those, and they helped me to feel positive about my recovery.

Over the next few days, Nana came in to look after me whilst Mom was at work because I was feeling so icky. It was great, because she really spoilt me; particularly when I was feeling at my roughest. In fact, I had been feeling so rough that I didn't even wait to pick up my usual treats before we left the surgery. (Can you imagine me being too ill for treats? I must have been feeling bad!) I was hopeful that I would get double treats when I went back in a couple of days. I knew my furry family would appreciate it and, knowing Doctor Brent, I was certain that he would make sure that we were properly looked after. And, if he'd forgotten that I'd missed out, I would just have to remind him politely.

It's a good job my family looked after me so well that week. Fortunately, the meds started to work and within a couple of days, I started to feel better. When I went back two days later, the Man with Pointy Things assured me that my snot was slowly clearing up and I was beginning to be able to breathe better. I still had a week of medicine left, but the Man with Pointy Things insisted it was all necessary to make me feel better - and then backed it up with a large bag of treats.

I have to say that the medicine was yucky; however, even though I still had some snot, it was going away.

However, as the weather got colder, my human brother and I staged a revolt and were very reluctant to leave our cocoons. As the weather dipped into negative degrees, I took my place on his bed and the rest of the zoo found their own spots for the day.

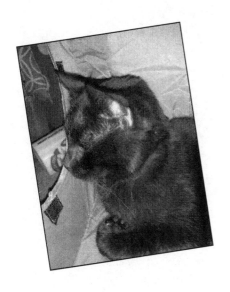

This was me on 16th January when I saw Mom getting everything ready for us to go out that morning. I knew I had to go back to see the Man with Pointy Things, but I had hoped that they would cancel public school, seeing as how my human brother attends one and my Mom works at one. But no; their advice was to dress "appropriately". For their information, there really is no appropriate wear for temperatures below ten degrees.

It was also the day when I had to go for my check-up. Mom had got the days confused, as she often does; it's not like she doesn't have to remember anything else. Fortunately, all school activities had been cancelled for that night because, again, there was no "appropriate" wear for this cold.

I have to say, I got the motherload of treats when I went back this time; however, because I still had some snot and some wheezing, the Man with Pointy things still wanted me to do a few days with kitty steroids to help with my breathing. And, because our vet is kind of cool, I allowed him to scratch me behind the ears and pet me. I could tell that he felt kind of honored by that privilege.

Mom and I also noticed that several of our cat friends here on this page had to make their own trips to their own Men with Pointy Things, so we said a little kitty prayer for them and their humans because, if they are anything like my Mom, we knew that they would worry until they were given the "all clear".

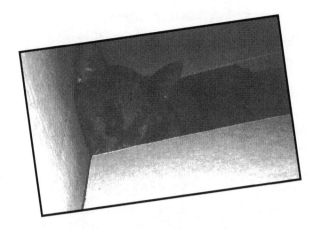

After a while, as I started to feel more like myself, I set up my own outpost in one of my favorite places – a cardboard box. Anyone who approached was promptly swatted and told to step back ... particularly as my appointment to return to the Man with Pointy Things grew close – although I guessed that, at last it was time for him to tell my humans that I was already good – which, of course, I already knew.

Fortunately, after shining a light up my nose and in my eyes; using a light to look in my mouth and a metal thing that he pressed to my chest so that he could listen to me breathe, the Man with Pointy Things determined that I was well. After this, he proceeded to pick me up and cuddle me and to talk to Mom about scheduling time for a dental check-up.

By the way, I have to say that this place is a little crazy. Every time we come, I meet new friends! This time, it was a little bitty dog who had hurt his paw. Naturally, Mom assured his human that they were in the right place and that he would be as good as new in no time.

My Human Brother

I was not the only one who was ill in January. My human brother had to visit his own Man with Pointy Things because he had a set-back from the flu, and he even had to spend a few days in hospital! I was quite shocked to hear that his Man with Pointy Things doesn't pet him, give him ear scratches or even provide treats for his patients! I guess that was why he had to take our Mom with him.

This meant that our human sister, Hayley, had to look after us for few days. That was kind of cool in some ways, because I love my human sister - but not so cool in others, because we all missed Mom and our human brother, Jax. We sent kitty prayers up for his quick recovery.


Nana and Pops came in from time to time to check on us as well. As you know, they spoil us rotten, and give the greatest snuggles, so we always like it when they come over. Also, I have to say, Pops is the greatest! One day, he was sitting there on the settee with the television on. Suddenly, I found myself on his lap, being petted. "I think you need to watch this film, Zero!" he told me. "These guys remind me of you!"

It was a wartime film called 'The Great Escape', and it was amazing! People were trying to escape from a Prisoner of War camp. I watched as one of the characters had 'time outs' in a little hut, and I noticed that his time outs were a lot longer than ours. I watched in awe as they dug – not just one, but *three* huge tunnels in order to make their escape and how they worked together to get as many people out as they could. "What amazing organization," I thought. If only I could rally my troops in the same way! But maybe their motivation wasn't the same and it was enough of a job trying to organize one tunnel – let alone three. However, the bit with the motorcycle looked like fun! If only they made motorbikes for cats!

The next day, my human sister heard that they were missing us too, so she snapped this pic of me to send to them. By that stage, I was really hoping that they would come home soon, as I didn't know how much more of Biscotti Gotti and Garcia Maria Lopez's whining I could listen to. Our human sister reckoned they just missed their other humans and assured me Mom and Jax would be back very soon.

You can guess how thrilled we all were when they both returned that evening. Although our human brother still didn't look all that well, they were both swarmed, and even I had to do a figure of eight round Mom's legs in greeting!

The whole of that night, Biscotti Gotti wouldn't get off Mom's knees and I couldn't see him letting go of her easily. I guess we do kind of need the humans that take care of us ... although that fact won't put me off all my digging. At least one tunnel will be dug by Spring!


Once they were back, I decided that it would be my job to help Mom to look after my human brother so, the very next day, he and I took over Mom's bed and TV and decided to spend the whole day there. I did explain to him that he had to keep his snot to himself, as I had no desire for another trip to the Man with Pointy Things. I had only just got over the last one! Nana came to help look after us, which meant that we were all spoiled rotten, because the woman simply can't say 'No'!

Over the next few days, we watched as our human brother slowly got better. He has asthma, though, which makes it hard for him to breath at times, so I moved onto his bed with him. I found that, if I rubbed my head on his hands or arms, he would put something in his mouth and, a few minutes later, he was feeling better. I was starting to be glad that I didn't have children of my own, because this was hard work!

Mom tried to help me out by peeking in throughout the night. As if I wasn't capable of looking after one human! I was a dictator, for goodness sake!

## February

Just 10 days after our human brother started to feel properly well again, it was my turn to feel not so hot. Once more, I was having mouth issues; it felt really sore, making me feel totally icky. Mom said, "Better safe than sorry," whatever that means and so she phoned the clinic. After a chat with someone called Amy, the Awesome Vet Tech, it was decided that I had to go in to visit the Man with Pointy Things again, just to make sure that it wasn't anything serious.

He and Mom were quite concerned, particularly as they really didn't know how old I was! I didn't know either, so I couldn't help them, but it seemed as though I was older than everyone had previously thought. As Doctor Brent put it to Mom, I was 'quite a distinguished gentleman'!

I was feeling so rough that my human sister and Mom made me this super comfy bed to snuggle up in. As it was cold, they even put a sweater on me to go and visit the Man with Pointy Things. I liked it so much, I didn't want to take it off! Judging from your comments, you all liked it too.

The medicine was yucky, as ever, but I had to take it twice a day. I just hoped it would work, because I really didn't feel very well at all, although I tried to be brave when Mom and I wrote my diary entry that night.

Dear diary
While I am not going to be dictating anytime soon, I am feeling a little bit better. Along with my new medicines, I have a new diet which seems to be easier for me to eat. At my last visit, my Man with Pointy Things said I had lost a few more teeth and, to top it all off, he said I was an older gentleman - his guess was probably around 10.

Apparently, there are pictures they could take of my bones; but he said he felt that was unnecessary and would upset me more than it would help. So, for now, it's lots of medicine and a new diet!

P.S.
I know why Biscotti Gotti loves his sweaters so much. Mom makes them super soft and warm, so I am not giving this one up anytime soon!

For the next few days, I really didn't feel like a dictator at all and Mom and I didn't post any comments – which concerned a lot of people. However, four days after I started taking the meds, I started to feel much more like myself; however, Mom announced that I still had a lot of medicine left. Not fair, I thought, but at least it seemed to be working.

My Man with Pointy Things called to check on me and to make sure that I was eating. Mom said that we were the luckiest because Dr Brent cares so much about his furry friends. All I can say is that I must love my new diet, because I leave a happy plate every time. Mom reckons that I will be as good as new in no time.

The medicine was still yucky but, according to everyone, I was already looking so much better, so I let them give it to me and got used to being thought of as 'a distinguished gentleman'.

Naturally, there were times when I decided that I was all better and had done with my medicine; but Mom's witchery lured me out every time.

When I hid under my human brother's bed, Mom cooed at me. "Who's a good kitty!" How did I, a dictator, allow myself to be fooled by that one? Witchery, I tell you! Witchery!

The next day, I decided to go up high to escape Mom's magic. Unfortunately, the mention of food and scratches lured me out again. I was starting to understand why Garcia Maria Lopez and Biscotti Gotti came running every time they heard that deceptively sweet voice. And they say black cats are deceptive? Their Moms are twice as bad! Mind you – I suppose they have to be, really!

## March

Of course, I was still on the meds. It seemed to be a long-term treatment where I was concerned now. I tried hiding again, and Mom kept luring me out with her witchery. The next time, it was those pawsome treats that our Man with Pointy Things gives us. Those things are like kryptonite – they momentarily paralyze you, so you lose all track of what you were doing, then ...!

However, after a fortnight of meds, I was definitely feeling more like myself again. I just had to wait for my check-up. Mom reckoned that I was looking better and eating better – we had to wait for the Man with Pointy Things to say the same thing – which, two days later, he did!

> Dear diary
> Guess who's back? That's right I am good as new. I have to go back again to the Man with Pointy Things in a week, but he says all is well.
>
> Mom asked if next time she could take a picture of

me and him, he said, "We'll see." I reckon that's code for 'yeah, you can.'

P.S.
It's cooler again so we are inside. Thank you thank you for all your prayers and good kitty vibes.

Zero.

But that wasn't the end of the story! A week later, when I went back for another check-up, they found a sore spot at the back of my mouth. Dr Brent, our Man with Pointy Things, thought that it was just an ulcer, which could be cleared up with more medicines (Yuck! As if I hadn't already had enough!) and steroid injections (Double yuck!). He said he wanted to see me again for more pets and snuggles when I'd finished taking the yucky antibiotics and that, if it wasn't better, he might have to take some special photographs!

Hmm! Snuggles, pets _and_ photographs! Some of my favorite things! That didn't sound too bad!

I continued taking my medicines, which Mom thought she disguised in the creamy broth and baby food combination that she gave me every day; mind you, if my clean bowl and my messy face were anything to go by, she wasn't doing too bad a job of it!

So, this was the new ritual: Every morning, I would sit and stare until someone fed me. Every so often, as I was staring, I saw the human add some kind of new substance to my food allowance, so I knew that she was up to her witchery again; however, I cleaned my bowl and allowed her to inspect it carefully to make sure that I had ingested everything.

Occasionally, Mom would take way too long to mix her potions; however, unfortunately I did not like waiting and rarely did so very patiently. From time to time, I may have had to remind her that I am a dictator and I demand my food rations in a timely manner! In return, she tried to remind me that it wouldn't kill me to have to wait occasionally; but that didn't go down too well with me. Dictator, I tell you!

After a couple of days, my Man with Pointy Things called to check that I was eating and taking all my meds. Mom was happy to be able to assure him that I was! I continued taking my other medicines as well, even though they were icky. Perhaps I could discuss the flavor with the Man with Pointy Things the next time I went, as it wasn't appealing to my palate!

Mom decided she would let everyone know her 'secret' recipe for getting me to take my meds. I still say it's all down to her witchery, though!

This is Zero's Mom.

For anyone who gives lots of meds like we do the recipe is:

- 1 jar of baby food (chicken, beef, ham, etc.)
- 1 package of cat broth or bisque (Petco (US) and Pets at Home (UK) have a wide selection.)
- Meds (as prescribed by the vet)

Mix together carefully and serve!

As always, check with your vet, but ours suggested this and it makes things so much easier for everyone

Misty

I have to say, Mom's witches' brews are certainly very good, and I do have a tendency to get bits of it on my face in my eagerness to eat it but, as Mom says, a clean bowl is a happy bowl, so no-one cares if my face is a bit messy.

## Yard Time

Of course, during the colder months, yard time was rare. When it was cold, we found things to do inside - including mischief - but, as soon as the temperatures reached 70 degrees or above, yard time was allowed!  This meant that digging could re-commence!  Remembering what I had learnt from the film I watched with Pops, I tried to rally my troops.

My sister from another mister, Garcia Maria Lopez, did some excellent work.  When Mom asked her what in the world she was doing, I told her to flash the puppy dog eyes and her 'I have absolutely no idea what you are talking about' look, but she was clueless!  Naturally, the humans filled in all our progress.

Personally, I was slightly miffed because, the entire time that my associates and I were digging, Edward Enigma was just lying in the sun on the outside of our prison. My goal was to find out how he managed to escape like Houdini! Unfortunately, in spite of my earlier hopes, he is still of no help to our cause!

One day, it was too windy for us to go out; but that didn't stop Pops from doing some things outside for us. He had some helpers: our neighbor's goats got out! We had great fun watching the humans trying to herd them back.

Before long, we realized that there was a good reason why Mom sticks to small animals. She really is no good at herding, which is good, as cats definitely can't be herded!

(By the way, I recently found out that 15th December is listed as International Cat Herders Day! Should I tell Mom that fact, do you think, or might it make her want to start trying even harder to do the impossible?)

## Cold Weather Fun

It can get very cold here in the winter – particularly in January, so there were frequent times when we didn't get to go out. Snuggles, snuggles and more snuggles! Our favorite hobby on cold days is snuggling – and there are plenty of friends – both human and furry – that we can snuggle with!

Sometimes, Mom would just open a door, so we could at least look out – which was all well and good until someone (Emmett Alexander) decided to just spread out in front of it. Even swatting him a few times with my paw, which is the universal cat code for moooove, didn't work!

Of course, we still enjoyed being good night kitties as well relaxed, cute kitties and tried to ensure that Mom posted our pictures regularly. For me, it was after had a long day of dictating. This was my "are you serious" face.

For my brothers, Emmet Alexander and Jasper Poe, it was when they were busy basking in the window because the sun was finally shining. It was finally a whole 36 degrees! We were hoping that we might even get to go out sometime soon! They became BFFF on the day Mom adopted Emmett Alexander. Jasper Poe just looked at him and said "A brother? Whatever! Cool!" and they were best friends from that moment onwards!

Arkham Darkham always looks at his cutest in the mornings. He is not really a morning person, and often gives a look as if to say 'I am not ready to begin my day yet. Go away!'

As for my sister from another mister, Garcia Maria Lopez, she just takes the 'cute puppy' look to another level! Mom and our human brother were just going to get a take-out but, naturally, she decided that she had to go too. One 'cute puppy face' later, and she got her own way! This was the result.

As ever, our elusive princess, Harley Quinn, was hard to capture; but, getting ready to sleep is always a good time, and she does look rather sweet!

When it comes to Biscotti Gotti, you just have to say 'photograph' and he poses in his cutest way! No wonder he gets away with, almost literally, murder! (I still want to know what he did with those poor ducks, and I'm sure I'm not the only one!)

## Operation Catnip

27th February 2018 was one of several Operation Cat-Nip Days organized in the Stillwater area. These are the day when people like my Mom volunteer to help to get cats and dogs checked in. They're also the days when vets like ours in various parts of the USA spay and neuter feral animals along with cats and dogs for low income families at a reduced rate because they're cool like that. Mom says that a lot of animal lovers come together to help to make this happen and to help to control the animal population. She says that many pet parents are educated on these days about becoming responsible pet people.

My human family managed to catch another feral friend this month, whom Mom and my human brother managed to drop off to help curb the animal population.

Our Man with Pointy Things participates in this several times a year, and Mom is always quick to help out too; you see, we hate the fact that so many pets are dumped and even killed. Our aim is that every pet that is born in the first world will be able to have a furever home where they will know love and care.

Operation Cat-Nip 2018 was a huge success. Two hundred and fifty feral cats along with animals belonging to families who couldn't afford spaying and neutering were provided with that, along with the necessary shots. Have I mentioned our Man with Pointy Things is 'the bomb' (as Biscotti Gotti phrases it!)? Dr Brent teamed up with a couple of vets and several techs volunteered their time and, from 7:00 am until late into the evening, they had the clinic open.

## Escape Gate II

One afternoon towards the end of March, some of my fellow prisoners escaped temporarily. Even though Garcia Maria Lopez had managed to start a rather impressive hole, they were all quickly recaptured and returned to their cells.

I must say, this attempted escape was not approved by me, seeing that I was still not allowed outside yet. Plus, I would absolutely not have stopped and smelt the flowers. Honestly! This was the sort of 'help' I had to deal with? It's not surprising I struggle at times!

I needed to think about how to organize my fellow prisoners to make a real bid for escape. Mom said maybe I should start watching 'Prison Break' whilst she was at work and get some pointers from there. Sadly, although I had found The Great Escape quite informative, I believe she was being sarcastic!

## My Best Friends

Apparently, someone on the Cat House page asked who my best friend was. Well, I am a very lucky cat, because I have two! Biscotti Gotti claimed me as his BFFF soon after we first met; and Garcia Maria Lopez has to me my best friend too, because she's a great hole-digger and a fantastic nap-sharer! She is definitely my sister from another mister!

I thought you might like to see this picture of her in her absolute favorite punk-rock outfit.

# Biscotti Gotti – My Brother from Another Mother

Of course, my other best friend, Biscotti Gotti carried on throughout the early part of the new year in his own, inimitable way. He destroyed a few soft toys and dolls and proceeded to hide numerous objects in his dog-cave place; some of which totally defeated all senses of logic. I mean, why hide unopened cans of cat food? Opened, I would understand. Unopened – well, that's two sandwiches short of a picnic in my opinion!

Naturally, he also still did daft things like getting caramel on his fur (the wrappers were found in his man-cave!) turning him into a sticky mess, which meant that Mom had to cut it out, as it was too bad for a bath. Fortunately, this time it was only on his butt and one of his paws, but Mom still wasn't happy – she said that she had been trying to keep his fur longer for the cold months. The groomer was happier this time: she always hated it when Mom had already shaped his beard. Biscotti Gotti, however, couldn't have cared less. He might have had a few clumpy places for a few days, but he would get to spend the day at the doggie spa, being pampered and spoiled and, to top it all off, he would be picked up by our Nana and Pops, who spoil us all rotten. Personally, I began to suspect that he did things like this on purpose.

As usual, he came back smelling April-fresh, and with his nails and hair done beautifully – but, by the end of the day, you could barely even tell that he had been groomed. That's so typical of him! He loves his spa days, but never manages to keep looking tidy for long! It's easier for us cats; we can all groom ourselves.

In March, Mom and my human sister, Hales, went shopping and found this amazing dog-coat; they thought that Biscotti Gotti HAD to have it! The humor was lost on Biscotti, but everyone else found it hilarious!

Needless to say, he wore it a lot over the next few months – if only to keep the rest of us amused.

# Chapter 9 - Springing into Summer

The next few months were very busy – as usual. Most of the time, I felt quite well; the weather was improving so we could get up to our normal antics; and Mom and I could write our observations, as usual. There were days when I would come in, exhausted after a rough day playing outside, eating and napping – and don't forget the treats and the toys – and be so tired that I would just have to find another place to sleep. Being a prisoner was hard work at times!

Then, there were the bad days! On my bad days, well, you know what it's like when you're feeling rough? Basically, a lot of time was spent with the Man with Pointy Things. And I wasn't the only one! My human brother, Harley Quinn and my canine brother, Biscotti Gotti all had to make visits – which, basically, meant even more of those yummy treats. Even appointments with the Man with Pointy Things have their advantages!

## Catnip and Eggs

One morning, we were extremely surprised to see our human family taking over the kitchen table. It looked as though they were painting eggs! We couldn't work out what was going on, but we left them to it. We didn't really want paint on our fur because we knew what the consequences would be.

The next day was a Sunday. They dressed up and went out to a place called Church – I'm not sure what it was all about but, when they got back, my human brother and sister disappeared into the garden for a while.

When they came back in, the door was opened and we were allowed out into the yard, where we found loads of little plastic eggs. My first thought when I saw these eggs was "Boy, does the chicken who laid those eggs need medical attention" – but then I smelled them ... and it all became really exciting because they smelled of catnip and treats!

As we found them, we nudged them, and they opened; giving us an amazing feast. Sometimes, they were a bit stuck, so the humans had to help us a bit, but the rewards were just as good!

Nana and Pops came over, and the humans had a delicious smelling meal. Naturally, we got to share some of it at ration time, and it was every good as bit as we had hoped. I have no idea what it was all about, but it was certainly a very exciting day.

It's a shame it doesn't happen every Sunday!

## Holiday Mischief

A week or so later, we were all in for a shock for a couple of weeks, as it seemed as though neither Mom nor our human brother were getting up. It appeared that they were having some sort of holiday! We were all slightly confused by this, as they were usually out of the door by 7.30 am – which is when our party would begin! However, all of a sudden, nobody was out of the door at all, hence the confusion. None of us could quite work out what was going on. It wasn't Thanksgiving or Christmas – so what was happening?

Rations were served rather late every day, which was even more disturbing. Although I tried to wait patiently, I felt that Mom needed me to remind her of her duties; after all, 5:30 was the time they should have been dispensed, and it just wasn't happening. It seemed to me that, because she did not have to wake early enough to get everything ready for work and to wrestle my human brother out of bed, she was falling behind. After a couple of days of this, I decided that I needed to have a proper word with her about it ... and some other things as well, such as Edward Enigma and his special privileges. She wasn't really listening, though, and just petted me gently, telling me what a lovely boy I was and that no one would starve if rations were a little bit late in the holidays!

By the fourth day, I even contemplated dialing 911, as any attempt to inform our jailer that our food bowls had still not been filled had gone totally unnoticed. I was beginning to fear that, if this wasn't quickly rectified, we would all perish. Perhaps I could persuade Jasper Poe to sing the song of our people until our struggle was taken seriously by the warden?

Eventually, after this had been going on for a few days, I sent Biscotti Gotti in to deal with her. As you know, I'm convinced that he was a mafia hitman in a former life, so he knows how to make his point felt. I got him to stand at the end of her bed and talk to her in a rather loud voice. She soon got up and fed us, although I wasn't even sure that her eyes were fully open as she did it! However, somewhat miraculously, we all seemed to get the correct rations – unlike the time when we had kept her awake!

The following day, further confusion ensued! The humans left, but later than normal, with lots of shouts of "Don't forget the signs!" and "Make sure you have everything!".

It turned out that there was an uprising in Oklahoma City; teachers and teaching assistants throughout the state were gathering together in some sort of protest – I didn't fully understand what was going on. All I knew was that someone, somewhere, had organized some sort of major revolution. I needed to see how it was organized in order to motivate my fellow prisoners – as this campaign was over 30,000 members strong. Imagine my kingdom with that many subjects! Oh, the holes that would be dug!

Naturally, while the humans were away carrying their signs, Biscotti Gotti took out yet more stuffed animals. He left a trail of stuffing to said animals. I know I have said it before – he might say he's my BFFF, but this one is a little sketchy! I was beginning to think that I needed to rethink my association with him. I tell you – former life – Hitman!

Then, Garcia Maria Lopez decided to betray me by becoming best friends with the master of Chaos, Arkham Darkham.

I decided that I had to regain control of my people. However, priorities had to be established. Nap first, then kingdom ruling … there again, probably several naps before kingdom ruling, as Biscotti Gotti is really is slightly off his rocker; some days, there really is no talking to him – and this looked like just one of those days!

# Mischief Making

Don't let my innocent face fool you! I, too, was quite capable of making mischief when I wanted to. The best part, of course, was trying to get away with it!

### Lego-Gate

13th April

In breaking news, I need to report that Zero Dark Thirty just took out the Lego Amusement Park!

The number of casualties is still not known.

Onlookers are saying that Biscotti Gotti was also involved in the incident, as several Lego Park goers are missing. It is feared that they may have met the same demise as the Christmas Ducks. Hope of rescue is dismal.

Emmett Alexander Out.

This was how my brother announced the situation on 13th April. In my defense, the humans were watching a trailer for the movie 'Rampage' and I believed that I could destroy stuff more effectively!

Needless to say, some of us had a time-out!

After consulting with the authorities (the Man with Pointy Things and Amy, the Awesome Vet Tech), Poop Watch 2018 began. For the next 48 hours, all poop had to be carefully inspected.

Eventually, all the Lego Park visitors were accounted for. Some were found in Biscotti Gotti's man/dog-cave but, sadly, others did not make it and were given a proper burial in the poop receptacle.


## Manners

One morning, I managed to start several fights with my brother, Emmett Alexander at ration time. I ended up in a time out 'until I could remember my manners when eating!'

I will remember my manners when Emmett Alexander remembers that I am in charge! Plus, time outs never last very long because Mom always forgets what we did! Double plus – time out is in my human brother's room, which has a memory foam mattress – not really a hardship!

Win, win situation!

On another day, I went up high to escape our

warden after starting a little kerfuffle! I may have known exactly what I was doing – I certainly heard Mom tell me that, more than once – but I got away with it, mainly because I can fit in places that she can't! Plus, I could still watch Biscotti Gotti and Arkham Darkham arguing from there!

Another win, win situation!


## Feather Toys and Dynamite Sticks

On several occasions, the humans would venture to the land of Petco to buy rations, treats, rubber chickens and even new collars, as one or other of us would 'lose' ours every so often!

One day, they went there to retrieve a collar for my canine sister, Garcia Maria Lopez. Somehow, they didn't come back with any collars, but they DID have bags of toys and treats – including one of our favorites – the dynamite stick!

I, however, was particularly enamored with a toy that dangled with lots of feathers. Mom's witchery was well and truly at work. Not only was she luring us with toys, but she scratched us, messing our hair and making it look crazy!

Unlike me, our resident Ninja, Harley Quinn, didn't know what to make of this feather toy. I was totally in awe of it! Mom just had to pull that thing out and I was mesmerized for hours!

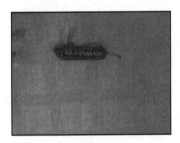

We all loved the dynamite sticks which Mom and our human family got us from time to time. They contain catnip, and they are amazing! However, this was what was left of the dynamite stick that Emmett Alexander and Arkham Darkham got their paws on one day!

As a result of this mischief, Arkham Darkham found himself in chair jail. I have to say, it could be a horrible confinement – not! All the humans walked past and scratched him on the head, telling him what a pretty boy he was! Of course, Arkham saw it as an opportunity to reach his paws out and snag whatever passed by!

## Yard Time

The weather started to improve, and so did the amount of time that we were allowed to spend in the yard – particularly after Mom's holidays had begun towards the end of May - after all, she had a lot of work that she needed to do out there.  Best of all (as far as I was concerned, anyway) the bird bath was back in my possession, where it was going to remain!
Once or twice, I had to voice complaints because my birdbath had water in it, but the problem was soon rectified!

Holes were dug: on at least one occasion, my whole crew were at work!  My hole was clearly still a hole!  Of course, Harley Quinn did her usual solo things, and Garcia Maria Lopez did her usual doggy things; sniffing and licking anything and everything seemed to be a a high priority for her.  When she did think about tunneling, she was an exceptionally good hole digger ... but she had too many other interests – and was all too good at drawing attention to the holes that she had dug!  I kept trying to remind her to hide them, but would she listen?

As for Biscotti Gotti, he continued to start numerous holes, but forgot that he was supposed to be tunneling and went on to do something else.  He is so easily distracted!

Arkham Darkham was rarely any use if you wanted help with escape plans but, if you needed grass or flowers to be sniffed, he was your man!

Pilgrimages to the Lowe's place (I'm told it's a major hardware store) had to be made, so as to obtain dirt and other hole filling materials – I know I've said this before, but Mom can be such a party pooper at times! On more than one occasion, unfortunately, the holes that we had managed to hide were uncovered. The dreaded hole filling supplies were brought out and made ready for use... just as I had got everyone organized and united! Typical!

As the weather got warmer, we may have got more outside time; but no-one felt particularly inclined to work. Water was put out for us to drink, and more water was put in our kiddie pool for us because we are weird, and most of us quite like getting our feet wet. As for Biscotti Gotti, he liked getting completely wet and shaking it all over everyone!

At times, catnip would be produced, and all progress on the holes would be stopped! Emmett Alexander, particularly, would be totally distracted. Then, one day, Biscotti Gotti and Garcia Maria Lopez found a turtle, which Mom had to relocate to a safer place. It could be really frustrating, being a dictator at times – and as for the escape plans ... well!

Sometimes, Mom even declared that there would be no yard time because it was too hot! I reminded her that I had lived in the heat before she gave me climate control which, although it was nice, would not deter me from my plans! VIVA REVOLUTION!!! However, Mom was firm on that point. If it was too warm for her, then it was too warm for us. As a result, yard time was mainly early mornings and late evenings ... unless the day happened to be a bit cooler!

# Introducing Bella and Corona and their Resting Place

Before any of us were adopted, Mom and the rest of the human family had two other cats: Bella Marie and Corona Elizabeth.

Mom always said that Bella Marie was the high-maintenance princess of the family – a bit like Harley Quinn; whereas Corona Elizabeth, her sister, was more of a tomboy, but they were both very much loved and very spoilt.

They came to live with my human family in 2008, having been dumped when they were barely weaned. (Apparently, Corona Elizabeth had been found in a Corona box; hence her name.) They ruled the roost until 2013 when, sadly, Bella developed cancer and died.

Corona Elizabeth missed her sister a lot and found it very hard after she had crossed the rainbow bridge. She hung on for long enough to get to know her new little brother, Jasper Poe (you can see him on the cupboards in this photo) but crossed the rainbow bridge around 6 months after her sister. They were both buried under the oak tree in our garden, which soon became a special place for all our family, human and furry.

At the beginning of June, the humans took time to redecorate their resting places. Although it was true that Jasper Poe was the only one who had ever met either of them, we had all heard about them, and their resting place was one of everyone's favorite places to sit in the sun!

Our human family had planted the rose bush, but the little tree just sprung up over them, giving them even more shade. It was a lovely place for them to rest.

Mom cried as she tidied that area – she always does. It seems that, however large our family may become, she will always miss those who have already crossed the rainbow bridge, just as they miss her.

## Back to The Man with Pointy Things

Of course, no month would be complete without a visit to the Man with Pointy Things for one or other of us.

# April

This month, my sister, Harley Quinn had to come with me when I went for my regular appointments. After speaking to Amy, the Awesome Vet Tech, it was believed that she had a cold, like the ones that I always got; but the all-knowing Dr Brent wanted to check her out.

Mom was very good at getting us into our pet taxis, although I was still not a fan. Every time I saw one, it reminded me of that horrible day and, although I know I had my furever home and my furever family, I still felt a bit nervous of them.

Mom knew that, so she used soft carriers and she would put our woobies in them – sometimes with a treat or two!  I would often run in, because I wanted the treats; plus, I did rather like the head scratches.  (Even though I might have claimed that I didn't, I think my little purrs gave me away!)

This time, I came back triumphantly with a handful of treats! Only one shot in my butt – although it was decided that I would have to pop back every two weeks to get another one.  I have to say that I didn't feel overly happy about that!

Poor Harley Quinn was not at all well, though. She got several shots and lots of meds. She wasn't happy and tried to sing the song of our people as loudly as Jasper Poe while Mom held her. I kept telling her that Dr Brent was great and that she would be fine, but I don't think she was listening.

Mom was told to bring her back in a week or, if she didn't start to get better, to bring her back straight away. Our Man with Pointy Things must have felt concerned about her. In the meantime, we were told that there would be more treats once Harley Quinn started to feel better.

She went back a week later and was given the 'all clear' - which was good; and a bucket load of treats – which was even better!

I still went back for my regular shots. I didn't like it, but the treats and the ear scratches were good.

## May

Not me this month! Although I was still getting my weekly shots, I was doing well again; but my partner in crime, Biscotti Gotti, went to the Man with Pointy Things to get his annual vaccinations in May. Anyway, that night, he started running a fever and puking, so Mom made the emergency 'phone call that no Mom of furry kids really wants to make. However, because Dr Brent is amazing, he told her to bring him in straight away, so she did.

It turned out that Biscotti was actually allergic to the parvovirus vaccine and it had made him really ill, so he got to spend extra time with you-know-who! Mom picked him up the following day, and he was almost straight back to his usual self. The decision was made that, in future, he would have to get shots before he gets his shots, if you know what I mean! Our family really do have the coolest vet in town!

# Chapter 10 – Feeling Ill

19th June

Mom here.

Zero Dark Thirty just wants to be a good-night kitty.

He was trying to wait patiently for his nightly rations. Unfortunately, it was very hot and humid here today, so no one went outside except for the dogs - and that was just long enough to their business and come right back in.

In other news, he got a new, flashy rainbow collar because, alas, he had lost yet another one! Fortunately, his tag numbers are recorded with the Man with Pointy Things, so no new tags were needed.

Speaking of the Man with Pointy Things, Zero will see him next week because, in enquiring about missing tags, I was reminded of his upcoming check.

I could see the look in his face as I made the appointment! He was clearly saying "Darn!"

Blame the responsible check-in lady, and the fact they know my furry family well.

---

20th June

Dear diary

My visit to the Man with Pointy Things has been moved to tomorrow. Apparently, I am drooling more than normal, and Mom wants to make sure there are no new issues with my mouth and teeth. So, 'of course they can fit me in', and 'of course it's no big deal.'

Well there had better be good treats and I might possibly let him give me scratches if he asks nicely.

Feeling disgruntled!

Zero.

What none of us knew at the time was that this was to be my last normal post, and that day was the last time I would ever be able to supervise my troops from the garden.

After that, everything rather rapidly downhill with my health; in fact, from my next trip to the Man with Pointy Things, I was never the same again.

It was the beginning of the end.

Mom took over the diary entries.

## 21st June

Good evening Cathouse people and furry friends.   Zero's Mom here.

Zero Dark Thirty needs some prayers tonight. Some of the shots he has to get made him sick this time, so he is going back in the morning and will probably stay the weekend with the person he insists on calling 'the Man with Pointy Things.'

After a full examination, including dental, it seems that unfortunately, he has lost 2 more teeth. As a lot of you know from my posts, we have a small zoo, but this little guy is special. He was dumped because of his medical needs and lived for a while on his own until he finally came to us.

Our vet is confident that he just needs a little extra love; his words not mine. Zero Dark Thirty's REVOLUTION LIVES!!!!

*    *    *    *    *    *

Of course, as soon as she started posting about my situation, hundreds of you commented. I felt your love and prayers coming in from all over the world – I was fighting, but I was also struggling, and I really didn't feel well at all.

\* \* \* \* \* \*

## 22<sup>nd</sup> June

Please keep my little dictator in your thoughts.

Dr Brent is keeping him overnight; and he said it would probably be for the weekend. The examination this morning showed that there is something in his throat. We didn't catch this on Wednesday because, for some reason, we usually don't usually do all the x-rays and photographs until August.

As I have said, I love all our rescued family members, but Zero is special. He lived a very hard life before he found his way to our backyard and eventually into his castle with climate control.

It was with tears in my eyes and hugs from all the staff that I left him in the very good hands of his 'Man with Pointy Things' and the wonderful techs and others who work for him. He said he would call later to tell us how he was doing and what his blood work showed today.

(Later)

Update on Zero Dark Thirty
He is getting lots of IV meds and fluids. More tests tomorrow. Someone asked if anyone would be there with him throughout the night. The answer is, yes. Our vet is amazing and keeps a

few techs who stay the night with furry friends when they need to be hospitalized.

Dr Brent said he would call first thing in the morning and let us know how he did. We will visit him in the afternoon.

Thank you, each and every one of you, for your kind words and your prayers.

## 23rd June

Good morning Cathouse friends.

I just spoke with our vet, and Zero Dark Thirty is doing better today. He is still getting lots of IV meds, but Dr Brent told me that our boy ate this morning and gave him head bops – always a good sign.

Today, he will get a few more pictures and lots of meds. The place on the back of his throat is an ulcer, but our vet feels it's not cancerous and, at this point, a biopsy would be very hard on him, so they are going to start a new med and see if that does anything. Keep sending him good vibes because they are working. We will visit him later this afternoon.

## 24th June

Hey Cathouse friends.

Zero Dark Thirty is still with his 'Man with Pointy Things'. Yesterday we visited him, and he was up and walking around and wanting his pets. Dr Brent said he has eaten again and is drinking; but he wants to make sure he is good before he can come home.

He is still getting lots of IV meds including steroids. The medicine for the ulcer in his mouth will take several days to see some improvement. Hopefully, Zero will get to come home tomorrow sometime.

Again, I want to thank everyone for sending Zero good thoughts and prayers. As soon as he is released, I will post lots of pictures. Sadly, yesterday we took none because we were more interested in snuggling him and making sure he knew we were not leaving him.

We are so blessed because, when we got there yesterday to see him, one of the techs had him wrapped in his woobie and was carrying him around to check on the other hospital guests. Yes, guests! That's what they call any furry friends who need to stay. So, keep sending pawsitive thoughts his way.

# 25<sup>th</sup> June

Hey Cathouse friends.

Update on Zero Dark Thirty.

Unfortunately, Mr. Zero will spend one more night with the 'Man with Pointy Things'. He has a couple more bags of meds that he will not finish until later tonight. He will get his blood drawn again and the morning and then he can come home with more meds.

Today, when we visited, he jumped out of his holding area and right into my lap for snuggles. Aside from a few shaved areas, he is very much the boy that we have come to love. I assured him we would be there to pick him up as soon as they said we could.

I cannot thank you all enough for loving our boy as much as we do. He's on the mend but still has a way to go. Unfortunately, until he is completely well, he cannot go out and enjoy the things he loves most. VIVA REVOLUTION!!!

# 25th June (later)

Today he got more IV meds and blood work. His 'Man with Pointy Things' also took a few more pictures of his mouth. He ate and drank while we were there and was being feisty – which was really good to see. He should be home late tomorrow morning.

He still has a way to go, but Dr Brent is pawsitive that, with time and lots of love, he will be back to his old self.

It was decided that, because he is having so many mouth issues, we will take pictures every 3 months, just so we know what's going on.

Again, thank you, every single one you for the love you have for this little rascal, I truly believe all of you had a hand in him responding to the medicine and giving him what he needed so he can come home. So many, many thank yous. VIVA REVOLUTION!!!!!!!

*   *   *   *   *   *

Then came the big announcement!  Mom was so excited – so was Biscotti Gotti (naturally).  Mom said he had been looking out for me all week.

*   *   *   *   *   *

## 26<sup>th</sup> June

Cathouse friends, Zero Dark Thirty is home!

Before he left the Man with Pointy Things, he had a little accident, so he had to get clean; which is why he looks a little frazzled in this photo.

Aside from missing some fur in a couple of places where he had his IVs inserted, he's still the same kitty. He will be sleepy for the next few days because he has been fighting hard to get well. He has new meds and we will follow up next week for a check up to make sure he is still doing well.

Unfortunately, Zero will be an inside kitty for the next month, doctor's orders. All of his furry family, along with his human siblings are very happy that he is home. Again, I cannot thank each one of you enough for all your kind words and loving our Zero as much as we do. And to all of you who have sick kitties or kitties who need a little extra know you are not alone while I may not comment on every one of you, I am cheering for all of them. VIVA REVOLUTION!!!!!!!!!!!!!!

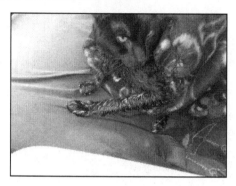

# 26<sup>th</sup> June - later

Zero Dark Thirty says good night. It's been a long day for him. He's currently being snuggled by his human sister who has declared he will be sleeping with her tonight. See you tomorrow Cathouse. Sweet dreams all my kitty army.

\* \* \* \* \* \* \*

But I was so very tired. I knew that my family would be well looked after and, however difficult it was going to be, I knew that it was time to stop fighting and to say goodbye.

Over the past couple of years, they had given me everything I needed – a name, a home, a family and (best of all) unconditional love. It was time for us all to move on and to let them share that amazing, unconditional love with others who needed it more.

Mom broke the news to everyone the following day.

# 27<sup>th</sup> June 2018

It's with a sad heart that I have to tell you, our beloved Zero Dark Thirty crossed the rainbow bridge early this morning. Our vet tried everything to save him, but his little heart gave out.

We cuddled him for a while before we came home, but it was hard to leave his little body behind, even though we know that Doctor Brent will look after him.

It will be a while before I post again. We are absolutely heart broken.

Misty

# Chapter 11 - In Mourning

29th June 2018

This morning, as I was sniffling because I remembered I have one extra food bowl; it was as though Zero Dark Thirty knew that I needed to laugh, because the elusive red maker (Zero's favorite laser pen toy) was brought to me by Garcia Maria Lopez. I decided to video both her and her brother Biscotti Gotti chasing it, because I could just hear Zero: "Biscotti Gotti, you can take out 3 baby dolls at one time, but you can't catch the red dot for me!" Even I had to laugh as I watched them try!

Late last night I started reading all your wonderful words, and our entire family has no words for the all the donations made for Zero. Not today or tomorrow, but I know somehow Zero Dark Thirty will let us know when it's time to let another friend into our pack. And we really are a pack. I have learned that the past couple of days. Garcia and Biscotti are always by me; Arkham Darkham and Emmett make sure there is still chaos in abundance; and then there is the very chill Jasper Poe who seems to know when one of us just needs to sit and pet him.

I said no more posting, but I swear it's like Zero is here telling me in a very dictator way, "Manage my troops, you crazy lady." I haven't read all the posts yet, because I can only get through about ten at a time, then I can't read any more through my tears.

This is my wish: if you have the chance to adopt a black cat, an older cat, or even a cat that just has been looked over, please do. Every last one of our furry family is someone who was discarded and left; yet somehow, once they chose us, we have slowly made this crazy family.

And, because my son is kinda brilliant sometimes, he said to me, "We should be outside. That was Zero's favorite thing, not inside looking out," - like I said, kinda brilliant sometimes. So, while I am sad beyond comprehension, we all go outside and watch Zero's brothers and sisters playing in the fenced in 'prison' that he loved so much, and we laugh, and my son and daughter say things that make us all smile and laugh remembering this hot mess of a cat who walked into our yard demanding rations, and never left.

Misty

\* \* \* \* \* \*

Your posts flooded in, showing Mom how much you cared about me, her and the rest of our wonderful family.

Meanwhile, back at the clinic, I was given a few last pets and snuggles from the Man with Pointy Things and his Awesome Vet Techs, before Dr Brent wrapped my body back up in my woobie and placed it in a special wooden box to be returned to Mom and the rest of the family.

# Chapter 12 - From Over the Rainbow Bridge

In the meantime, from my place beyond the rainbow bridge, I watched the family carefully and noticed how, every single time Biscotti Gotti went outside, he would find that particular spot in our enclosed area where I often laid when I wasn't in my bird bath, and would circle it, sniffing it as though I were still there ... which, in some ways, I was.

I saw how Mom still cried because she missed me, and the other members of the family looked for me at times.

Eventually, because Mom was too upset to do it, Pops collected my box from the clinic and got everything ready. I watched from beyond the rainbow bridge as my human family laid me to rest by my sisters, Bella and Corona, underneath the big oak tree, and placed a stone on top that read 'Best Battle Buddy Ever'.

Mom cried for me and for all the other kitties that have mattered to us and have left us ... and she left the last hole that I supervised without filling it in because she reckoned that, as long as no-one could escape through it, it would be a reminder of me.

Edward Enigma came to spend time with me most days. He would tell me that everything was OK, and he was watching out. I knew all was well, but I still had some work to do from beyond the rainbow bridge before I could finally relax.

After I had been across the rainbow bridge for a little while, I felt that I had explored it thoroughly; but I knew that Mom and the rest of the family were still missing me, so I kept sending them messages. Little ones at first, then bigger ones.

First, I gave my human sister a dig and got her to take Mom along to a rehoming day. You see, I happened to know that there was a pair of kittens there who would be perfect for the zoo – and that one of them was the ideal next dictator in training, the next one to help bring order to the chaotic household that I had left behind. I also knew that, if Mom didn't take them, they would be separated and would never achieve their potentials.

Lo and behold, off they went – and, as I had planned, they fell in love with the two kittens I had sent them to see. They were bonded brothers – one, quite timid; the other fairly bold; but it was the timid one that I was most interested in. You see, I knew he had the strength of will and character that was needed.

Labrinyth Dark Thirty and Castiel Jude Novak became part of the family and, once he found his feet, Labrinyth took over as the new Dictator in Training.

Next, I whispered something into Mom's ear about the revolution continuing, and about how it needed a special day to celebrate it. After all, isn't every great revolution celebrated with a special day? Think of July 4th – Independence Day; July 14th – Bastille Day in France. I'm sure there are many more if we were to look into it. Anyway. our revolution needed a day too.

Saturday August 4th was chosen to be the first ever Zero Dark Thirty Day.

I loved it – I had become a famous Revolutionary Leader in my own right, and even had a day named for me! What dictator wouldn't be happy with that idea?

People all around the world were encouraged to visit their nearest cat or dog refuge center; to volunteer and to spend time with the animals; to cuddle them and pet them; and even to adopt if they could.

It was absolutely amazing! Watching from beyond the Rainbow Bridge, I saw so much happening! I saw a senior dog named Teddy, whose tongue hung out just like mine, get a forever home. People who had never walked a dog did so for the first time in their lives; cats and kittens were adopted; so much was happening! And all the time, Mom was urging everyone on with pictures of me and campaign speeches worthy of Winston Churchill, Britain's famous wartime Prime Minister himself!

However, my family were still missing one member. I kept watching Biscotti Gotti sitting on our little seat in the window, waiting for me to come home. He clearly didn't understand that I was never coming home again – not in my usual form. I even heard him crying quietly when he thought no-one was looking, and he needed even more cuddles from the humans than normal. He was obviously missing me a lot – and I knew that I was missing him too.

After a few weeks, things started to improve for him, but he still spent time on our seat, watching out for me. I knew that I had to do something about it. He needed a new little black panther to befriend, a new BFFF; and one was coming their way, courtesy of Edward Enigma. For a while, he kept introducing new cats to the feral feeding area; but then I gave him one special little one to take along – a small, feisty, black kitten with massive, bat ears. Initially, Mom thought he would be part of the feral colony, but I had other ideas. This little boy had a role to fill in our family!

It took a few days for him to really trust the humans but, just as it had been with me, it was the girl, Hayley, who captured him and brought him into the zoo.

Apparently, someone had joked that I had put a lo-jack on the house, directing all lost kitties there; and so that became his name – Lo-Jack Blue; the next member of the family – the panther that would make the house feel complete again.

Although I know that Lo-Jack has not replaced me as Biscotti Gotti's BFFF, he has helped my friend not to feel so sad and to realize that life goes on. He doesn't spend as much time at the window looking out for me nowadays but, whenever he goes there, Lo-Jack is with him too and you can often find them comforting one another. As I said, he had a role to fill, and he is doing it!

However, I still knew that that my family were still missing me; there was one more thing that I needed to do for them so, eventually, I sent them this letter to reassure them that all was well with me. I wanted them to know that, although I miss them a lot, I am happy here and can still lead our revolution from beyond the rainbow bridge!

Dear family
I miss you all so very much, but I want you to know I am happy and healthy. I have a new garden with a different birdbath; it's almost as good as the one I had.

I met my sisters Bella and Corona and they wanted you to know that they miss you too, but they know we will see each other again one day.

I was sick Mom, as you know, and I was tired; so very tired. I know you did everything you could for me, but

I also knew you would keep fighting for me so, while we were sitting in the room with the pink curtains, I decided for you. Even as you were driving me frantically back to the Man with Pointy Things, I had already chosen. So even though you and he and everyone else was trying everything they could do to save me, it was time.

Please know, I still come and go as I please, and I am still watching over all of you. You were my family and you loved me, which was all I ever wanted. So, while I know you are all sad, don't be. Keep going what we have started, keep helping those who are helpless, keep encouraging people to do things.

You were my people because I chose you, and a better family I couldn't ask for. Give Biscotti Gotti some extra love, especially on those days when he is looking for me. And, woman, you really should fill in that hole, it's gotten to be quite impressive.

I'm good here, Mom, so you don't have to worry about me.

VIVA REVOLUTION Mom.

Love,
Zero Dark Thirty

# Chapter 13 – Interviewing the Zoo

Mom still had a lot of ideas for making my name live on. She and Elaine had already gotten together to create this book, and then they had this 'great' idea. Why not get the zoo to talk about me – what they thought about me, how they miss me and so on!

Not too bad an idea, I thought – as long as they say nice things! So, Mom was kept very busy for a few days, cornering the various members of my crazy family and interviewing them

\* \* \* \* \* \* \* \*

## Arkham Darkham

Mom: Arkham can I ask you a few questions.

Arkham Darkham: Yes, Mommy dearest. Wait! What kinda questions because I know nothing about those Smarties that Garcia Maria Lopez had.

Mom: What Smart..., never mind. I want to ask questions about Zero.

Arkham Darkham: What about Zero, he was my arch nemesis, you know.

Mom: Yes, you and Zero had your differences.

Arkham Darkham: Differences! He tried to tell me what to do and he laughed at me when I sat in those lovely little boxes!

Mom: Yes, but secretly I think you admired him.

Arkham Darkham: If, by 'admire him' you mean doing everything he said not to, then absolutely.

Mom: Really, Arkham?

Arkham Darkham: Ok, the truth is I just liked messing with him. When you told us that he was not ok, I was really sad.

Mom: See, I knew you really loved him.

Arkham Darkham: Of course, I loved him, he was my brother and you say we don't always have to like to each-other, but we do have to love each other. Hey. Mom, you might want to check the dog-cave?

Mom: Why? ...Biscotti Gotti, where did you get that candy?

## Emmett Alexander

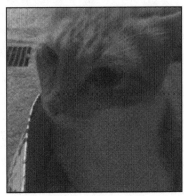

Mom: Hey Emmett do you think you could step out of the box so I can ask you a couple of questions?

Emmett: Why do I need to be out of the box?

Mom: Because I would like to see your face properly and it's not easy with you down there.

Emmett: Ok, fine, but make it quick. I don't need Arkham thinking it's his turn in the box.

Mom: Can you tell me about Zero?

Emmett: Well, perhaps our first meeting was not great. I may have mentioned his tongue and he may have commented on my lack of a tail.

Mom: But you guys worked out your differences?

Emmett: Yeah, I guess so.

Mom: What do you mean, I guess so?

Emmett: Well you made the rule that, and I quote, "You don't always have to like family, but you will love them and respect them."

Mom: (In that special tone of voice that the family all know!) Emmett...

Emmett: Nah, I had respect for him. I mean he never did any work; he got everyone do it for him. He was a good brother. The one thing I never understood, though, was having a dog for a best friend - especially Biscotti Gotti! I mean, really, what kind of friend eats your toys? Can I be done now?

Mom: Sure, I wouldn't want to keep you any longer from your box.

## Edward Enigma

Mom: Edward Enigma - you got a minute?

Edward Enigma: For you, I guess.

Mom: I feel privileged!

Edward Enigma: Lady, you know I am a busy man.

Mom: I know, I know. I wanted to talk to you about Zero. Maybe you could tell me a little bit more about how you found him?

Edward Enigma: Zero! Woman, that cat had no clue about living on his own. If I hadn't found him, who knows where he would have ended up? I don't think I've ever seen such a miserable looking ball of fur in my life as I did that day!

Mom: So, you just took him under your wing, no questions?

Edward Enigma: Well yeah, you saw him when I first brought him to you. Kid was kinda scared of his own shadow and didn't trust anyone. I told him you guys were good people. Did he believe me? Nope! Took him a while but I knew he was destined for something better.

Mom: What about you Edward? I think you're pretty amazing.

Edward Enigma: You know my job. I lead strays to you guys and to others around here. If I think they need it, I help them find a furever home nearby. Zero had his purpose too, and you guys helped him do it. I miss that kid.

Mom: I do too, Edward. I wish we could have had more time.

Edward Enigma: I know, but I also know you guys gave him what he wanted more anything: a family of his own.

Mom: I love that you stop by his tree most days. What do you tell him?

Edward Enigma: Just that I'm keeping watch, and all is good!

Mom: That's nice. You know you could always come in as well.

Edward Enigma: I know, but you also know I like coming and going as I please.

Mom: I know you like your freedom. Besides who else is going to bring all the strays?

Edward Enigma: Plus, no offense, but I've seen what Biscotti Gotti can do! That dog is slightly off his rocker!

Mom: See ya later, Edward!

Edward: Yeah. See ya later.

## Biscotti Gotti

Mom: Biscotti Gotti, I want to ask you some questions.

Biscotti Gotti: I don't know nothing about nothing. Do I need legal representation? There's a lady who's always offering legal advice on that page you go on. Something about a catturney? Do they help dogs too?

Mom: Biscotti what are you talking about? You need what ...? Never mind, I want to ask you about Zero.

Biscotti Gotti: Zero! Zero was my bestest furry friend forever. (Wags his tail happily.)

Mom: How did you get to be his best friend?

Biscotti Gotti: Bestest, Mom, and duh I just decided.

Mom: So, what made you decide?

Biscotti Gotti: Well he didn't have any friends, so I just decided. I knew he needed a friend.

Mom: So, what was your favorite thing about Zero?

Biscotti Gotti: He was a good nap taker. Plus, he always shared his treats. But, mostly, he was my friend. I keep looking for him, but you said he ain't ever coming back and that makes me sad.

Mom: Me too, Biscotti. I miss that mad little cat. (She picks him up and puts him on her lap.) So, are you ever gonna tell me what happened to those ducks?

Biscotti Gotti: Ducks? What ducks? I have no idea what you are talking about, and I know absolutely nothing about any candy that might have disappeared either!

## Garcia Maria Lopez

Mom: Garcia Maria you got a mad minute?

Garcia: For you, Mommy, always.

Mom: That's my sweet girl. Can you tell me a little about Zero?

Garcia: Zero? He was strange at first. He always looked like he was going to blow raspberries on someone, but he was OK when you got to know him.

Mom: He was your brother, but you two argued some.

Garcia: Well yeah. He constantly tried to tell me how to dig a hole. I am a dog, I assured him that I knew how to dig a hole. It's my job to dig holes!

Mom: He constantly spoke of freedom.

Garcia: Mom, that cat wasn't going anywhere! He just liked to boss us around and pretend.

Mom: Well he was a dictator!

Garcia: Yeah, well, he'd never have survived out there for long. He was a good brother, though, and I miss him. He was a great nap buddy!

Mom: I miss that crazy boy too.

## Harley Quinn

Mom: Harley Quinn you think you can stop scowling for a minute?

Harley: What could you possibly want?

Mom: Can we talk about Zero?

Harley: Zero? What do you want to know?

Mom: Tell me about your brother?

Harley: He was kinda awesome. I mean I work in stealth; he just meowed his orders and the others listened!

Mom: Tell me about him and Biscotti Gotti?

Harley: Oh, good grief, those two knew nothing about stealth. They were loud and constantly plotting something. Only one problem: Biscotti Gotti has the attention span of a toddler!

Mom: What about you and Zero?

Harley: What about it? I talked to him when I wanted to. He knew I was never going to listen to him, so it worked out well for everyone. I do miss him, and I get kinda sad when I see Biscotti sitting and waiting for him. Those days I try to be a little nicer, for his sake.

Mom: I think we all miss his bossiness.

Harley: Yeah, he was one of a kind.

Mom: That he was.

## Jasper Poe

Mom: Jasper Poe what's up?

Jasper Poe: Oh, you know chilling and contemplating life.

Mom: Can you tell me about Zero?

Jasper: Zero really needed to learn to relax. I mean dictatorship is stressful. I tried to get him to just sit back and watch and enjoy the chaos.

Mom: Not really a Zero thing.

Jasper: No not really a Zero thing. He was made to give orders. Me I just sat back and watched. What confused me was Biscotti Gotti and him being best friends. But, for whatever reason, they got along.

Mom: Yeah, they were a strange pair for sure!

Jasper: Yeah, they were definitely an odd couple; but Biscotti was Zero's first real friend, so it made sense really.

Mom: Yeah, our little Hitman was sweet that way. Always making sure Zero knew he was part of our crazy family.

Jasper: Crazy is right, that's why I am going to go back to meditating and watching.

Mom: Thanks Jasper, I love you, kiddo.

Jasper: Back atcha, Mom! (Head bumps against Mom's leg!)

# Chapter 14 - It's not the end

My plaque at Cat House on the Kings was unveiled in December 2018 – what an honor!  My life on earth may be over ... but my revolution will continue until every animal has a furever home.

Our family just wanted to take a moment to thank you all for welcoming us into your lives for a while. We shared our stories over time because we were funny people who had funny adventures; but we also shared them so that people could see that, even though some of us were a little different (and some of us were dogs) you can make a pretty great family out of rescues and the animals like myself and Biscotti Gotti who were literally thrown away. So, while I hope that I made you laugh and smile, I also hope that, after seeing me and reading this book, you consider adoption or rescuing. Mom always says that the greatest animals are the ones just one person believed in and loved. So, if you are considering a pet, whatever kind it may be, think about giving an animal a second chance or take a chance on that feral cat who, like me, might just need the right person to show them kindness.

What our family would like people to know is that it's not ok to leave helpless animals who have no way to defend themselves without protection; and it's certainly not ok to abandon any animal - big or small, young or old. There are many places that will take them and re-home them.

So, adopt – don't shop - for pets. There are many of us out there and, who knows? You could end up with a Zero, or your own Harley Quinn; an Emmett Alexander, or a Jasper Poe, and we can't forget Arkham Darkham! And, of course, no family would be complete without a former mafia hitman like Biscotti Gotti, or a best friend like Garcia Maria Lopez

Zero Dark Thirty

#VIVA REVOLUTION!!!!

## Messages from Mom

> Grief never ends ... but it changes. It's not a passage, nor a place to stay. Grief is not a sign of weakness, nor a lack of faith ... it is the sign of love.
>
> Author Unknown

I am aware that many of you who read this book may have had their friends cross the rainbow bridge recently. Recently, I saw this and thought it was fitting.

Grief does indeed change. It goes from absolute heart break to something different. I have realized it was not a permanent place. Do I miss Zero Dark Thirty any less? Absolutely not, but the grief now is just a sadness because I am selfish, and I would have done absolutely everything to keep him just a little bit longer. He made the final choice for us; unlike me, he knew that this overwhelming sadness was just a step in the process.

Letting a member of our furry family go is the price we all willingly pay to be able to love them. And, because grief changes, we pay the admission again and again, because that's what love is. It's a beautiful never-ending circle, and grief and loss are just one part. My heart goes out to each and every one of you. This place you're at right at this moment is just a stop because the circle never ends.

Dear Zero

Rest easy now, I'll take the next watch.

You started out with someone thinking you were nothing, but you have inspired an entire group of people around the world and, most importantly, you lit fire in your family.

Do feel free to stop in and let me know you're good, because we miss you so very much.

Mom.

# Appendices

1) Zero's Day

2) Zero's Box

3) Zero's Book

4) Some of the Charities we hope to support through sale of this book.

## Zero's Day

After the idea that I whispered to Mom took shape, the first ever Zero Dark Thirty Day was held on Saturday, August 4th, 2018. People all over the world went out of their way to do things for abandoned cats and dogs.

Some took food and blankets to their local vets, or to a local sanctuary; some visited and spent time with animals that had been considered unwanted; yet others actually used the day to offer an animal a 'furever' home. Mom was totally overwhelmed with all that she heard and was thrilled by what an amazing day it had been.

Me – I had never been in any doubt about it! It was my idea, after all!

Mom posted the following, and several other comments like it, in the month leading to Zero's Day, and many of you responded!

There are so many different ways you can make a difference on August 4th. Feed some ferals, heck you are a true warrior when you can trap one, I have first-hand knowledge of this (Edward Enigma was probably one of the hardest I've ever had to catch!) Donate, advocate, educate, foster, rescue. Money is crucial but so is your time because most of these rescues run on volunteers. Volunteers who clean cat boxes, walk dogs, play with the animals, foster the animals etc.

Zero Dark Thirty VIVA REVOLUTION!!! Saturday August 4

No matter how small or insignificant you think your actions are, I am telling they matter. They matter to animals that have been abandoned, forgotten, discarded. My daughter jokes I like the animals more than people sometimes. Sometimes she's right, animals love straight forwardly without complication. So, VIVA REVOLUTION!!!!! VIVA my little dictator!!!!!!"

Someone asked why August 4?

Honestly, I don't know. All I can think is that it was Zero! There I was, sitting, writing in my calendar everything that needed to be done before we go back to school and, I kid you not, something just said, "On August 4th you are going to go spend all day playing with animals and you should get other people to do the same." So, before I even realized what I was doing, I was writing Zero's day. And it just clicked! Absolutely, encourage people to go out on this day to honor and remember Zero Dark Thirty, but maybe, just maybe, find some furever homes for others, and just LOVE.

In the end that what it comes down to: LOVE. LOVE for each other, LOVE for the lost, just plain simple LOVE. So, go out on this day and love so big your heart hurts, and your face hurts from smiling and laughing. Adopt, rescue, donate, and give a little time, because when you do any of these you have LOVED.

Help me show the world what one little black cat who had been discarded has inspired.

I am rallying your troops my little dictator. Oh, how I miss you.


VIVA REVOLUTION! What does that mean?

It means, as Ghandi said, "Be the change you want to see in the world."

What I want more than anything is that every rescue, shelter, animal welfare, any place that houses animals of any kind be a No-Kill House.

With me sharing Zero Dark Thirty, people got a glimpse of what it was like to have a cat with special needs; a cat that somebody just decided to dump on our dirt road. I can't fathom the number of Zeros who have been left like him. If nothing else, please educate people about having a pet and the responsibility because, as you know, it's like having a toddler most days! Our whole family learned so much from Zero. We learned to be a little more patient, we learned to laugh a little louder.

No animal should ever leave this world without knowing what it feels like to be loved unconditionally. Zero left us knowing how much we loved him and how much we were going to miss his cute little face. That's what I hope that 4th August is; a start so every single animal that's abandoned, discarded can know someone cares.

Misty

Happy Zero Dark Thirty Day!!!!!

Everyone went off to do their bit – including Mom and my human brother and sister.  It was a busy day for them ... and for many more of you!  In fact, as Mom said, you went out in droves! Some of you donated money; others, time; still others, supplies; and some of you did what Mom and I had hoped.  You fostered, you adopted; and you gave furry friends a furever home!

Mom was thrilled – and her heart was full, because so many little souls were going to experience love and mercy – because the revolution lived!

5th August 2018

Cathouse friends, you guys killed it today. There was everything from card making, to feeding ferals, to a few who played with dogs for the first time and taking food to those who needed it. You name it I think it was done today. So many, many thank yous.

This is my hope: the first Saturday in August is to be Zero's Day; a chance for people everywhere to do what they can with what they have. You guys are an amazing group of people and Zero Dark Thirty may have inspired this day, but the rest was you all. To all of you who adopted today, and those who signed up to foster, I applaud you. Today know you were the heroes in this story, I was just a woman who loved a black cat and wanted to honor him. So, thank you each and every one of you, you were game changers today. VIVA REVOLUTION!!!!! VIVA ZERO DARK THIRTY!!!!!

Misty

In fact, she was so stoked, so impressed by all that happened that, three days later, she upped the game by encouraging anyone who could and who wanted to, to drop off used towels and blankets to their local shelters and rescue centers. As she pointed out, the animals come in scared and nervous, just like small children; and these things can provide a sense of comfort and safety.

I know that all my brothers and sisters and I had our very own special blankets – Mom called them our woobies – and we had our own special places for them.

Again, you went off in your droves, and many shelters were thrilled to receive 'woobies' for their rescues.

The joy of Zero's Day went on and on. Mom was thrilled, as ever! She couldn't believe how well it had all gone. As for me, I kept telling her that she should have trusted me … especially as I have a few more ideas that I'll be pushing her way over the next few months! (Bruhahaha)

---

16th August 2018

There has been great loss and I completely understand but because of great loss something amazing has been put into motion.

Zero Dark Thirty has inspired people to do something.

I want all of you to know that, while people are sad, and I am sad, great things are going on. Every single day I get a message about something someone has done and how this crazy little black cat called them to action.

People aren't sitting on the side-lines anymore. I cry every day, usually at morning rations when I have one empty bowl, but then out of nowhere; it's like Zero is there telling me there's still things to do.

Remember this; because of our Zero Dark Thirty, so many animals are being helped. I truly believe, besides loving us his family, this was his reason to be here, he knew he would be a game changer; he just needed someone to believe in him. So, while I am sad, I am also excited because great things are happening and will continue to happen because Zero lit a fire and it's my duty to make sure it stays burning.

I can tell you that I visit Zero and his sisters who went before him, and it's so peaceful. He's good and happy, sitting in his birdbath and bossing everyone around. So, while I know there is great sadness right now, I can tell you unequivocally Zero is happy and healthy and at peace and still keeping watch even though I have told him I'll take the next one.

I wish all of you, peace and comfort and, while our family is still heartbroken, we have made it our mission to make sure every single animal is not forgotten. You amazing, wonderful people are doing just that. You guys went out in droves because of a black house panther, and every day you guys are changing things. While there is sorrow, sometimes beyond my comprehension, there is also unbelievable mercy and grace.

So, to all of you grieving, know there is peace. For me, it comes out if nowhere and usually when I just need a little push. Just be still and know that, even though our furry family has gone on to a better life, they're still hanging out; because we are human, and we need direction - who better to guide us than cats?

Love to each and every one of you,

Misty

## Into the future

I am happy to be able to announce that the first Saturday in August has now officially become Zero Dark Thirty Day – the day when my wonderful, amazing family asks everyone who is able to do so to go out and volunteer or donate.

If you haven't done so already, why not go and have some fun playing with some awesome animals every year!

# Zero's Box

Mom and Nana were very busy for a few weeks, creating something very special that they could send off to Cat House on the Kings – something that would help them to raise money to help more cats like me. She heard that they had received an influx of little cats that needed a lot of medical attention and was determined to do her share.

After Nana had her stroke, whilst she was in hospital, Mom was even more determined to send the box off; not because she thought it would be the last thing they did together – she was very optimistic that Nana would soon recover – but because it was yet another thing that she had been able to do to help others.

She was really excited as she packaged up all the things that they had created and put them in a box – which she then entrusted to the US Mail Service. Expecting it to arrive in the next couple of days, she teased all the readers of my Secret Diary with a video as she took it to the mail.

The next day, she teased everyone a bit more – mentioning that she hoped 'her little dictator' would be everywhere! You were all really intrigued!

In the meantime, she was tracking the box, and was really excited when the message came to say it had been delivered ... then the shock came! The box had NOT been delivered – or at least, not to the right place.

Messages were flying all over the place and numerous posts were made on the Cat House on the Kings Facebook page. Mom and the rest of the Cathouse community were on fire, and even the babies were concerned. Little Labrinyth posted his worries on the page and tried to comfort Mom with purrs and snuggles.

However, other friends had faith in me. As they pointed out, if I could send kittens to new homes, surely, I could help the box to return to its rightful destination. But it seemed to be a big job, even for me and all my helpers across the rainbow bridge.

An inquiry was started.

Mom posted the tracking number; the phone number for the local Post Office at Parlier; and even an email address for Postmaster there. She then got the Cathouse Community to help her to campaign for the return of the parcel. After all, this wasn't just any old package – this was my box!

Some people were really concerned about what was in the box – a rumor began that it was my ashes; however, Mom pointed out that I was carefully buried under the oak tree with my sisters. She assured them that it was filled with handmade goods to honor me and to help the cathouse. It was insured – but the insurance was irrelevant – she wanted the goods delivering to the right place!

After two days, Mom was getting desperate. Many calls to the Post Office had been made, and e-mails had been sent from all over the world. Never had a delivery had so many enquiries made about it! I reckon if they had known what Team Zero was like, they would have taken more care with it in the first place!

Anyway, to cut a long story short, the box finally turned up at Cathouse nine days after it was posted – and, the following day we were able to finally reveal what had been in it as well as telling you how you could get your hands on one of your very own!

21st September 2018

HATS OFF TO ZERO DARK THIRTY! 🖤

Misty Bridges-Vaverka has created some wonderful hats as a fundraiser for The Cat House on the Kings. This is a LIMITED EDITION ~ when they run out, they're gone!

Heidi Stabbart was the first one to post her own picture of one in use!

As Cathouse said – Hats Off to Mom and Nana!

# Zero's Book

My next idea was another gentle nag – supported by some of our friends on Cat House.

"Write a book, Mom. Put our story in a book!" I kept telling her. Other people helped me by commenting as she posted. "You need to put these diary entries onto a book, Misty. They're amazing!!" you told her; but she wasn't sure. She wasn't confident – she had never written a book and didn't think she could do it; but I knew there was someone there who could help her, so I drifted over the Atlantic to the UK. You see I knew that one of the people who read our diary regularly was a writer who had already written several books.

For weeks, I sat on the corner of her desk, watching her work. Before long, I knew she was the one who could help us.

A few more nags in a range of directions, and the messages started flying between Mom and Elaine. My book had started! I was really excited, because I knew that this was another way that we could help other cats like me. If people bought my book, we could raise money to help Animal Rescue Charities around the world.

I kept sitting on Elaine's desk while she was writing, helping her to tell my story in my words. Mom kept sending her ideas through too and, before we knew it, my book was on its way!

I have to say that I was a bit of a slave driver at times! Elaine kept telling me that it was after midnight – but I was on Oklahoma time, so it was still only the early evening! However, she knew how eager I was to complete my book, so she worked incredibly hard and got really good at listening to me too.

As a result, here is my book and here is my story – some of which was never told in my diaries.

I am pleased to be able to say that all the profits made on this book will be donated to animal charities – particularly to Cat House on the Kings in California and to Operation Cat-Nip in Oklahoma – so they will be able to help other cats like me.

With lots of love to all of you from across the rainbow bridge,

Zero.

# Charities

Here are some of the charities that the money raised from the sale of these books will go to help.

---

## Cat House on the Kings

For more than 25 years, The Cat House on the Kings has been rescuing and saving tens of thousands of cats in central California.

Located on 12 beautiful acres next to the scenic Kings River, the Cat House on the Kings is a non-profit organization ~ a No Kill, Cat Rescue and Sanctuary. They receive absolutely no government funding and rely solely on donations from animal-loving people who share our vision about cats.

In addition to rescuing cats, they've been facilitating low-cost spays and neuters for community, stray, owned and feral cats for more than a quarter of a century!

Since its founding 25 years ago by Lynea Lattanzip, The Cat House on the Kings has saved over 30,000 cats and 7,100 dogs (not counting the 56,000 animals they have spayed and neutered!) and currently cares for more than 700 cats and kittens, a dozen or so dogs and dozens of peacocks.

Their mission is to:

- Provide a no-cage, no-kill sanctuary for feral and abandoned cats and kittens for the State of California, primarily serving the Central Valley;

- Facilitate the adoption of cats (primarily), dogs and other rescued animals into safe, loving, healthy and permanent homes;

- Educate the public on how to become directly involved in improving the quality of animal welfare;

- Offer low cost spay and neuter referrals

## Operation Catnip Stillwater

This charity is based in the nearest town to Misty's home, and is a charity that is close to her heart. It is also one that her Man with Pointy Things is very involved in.

Operation Catnip, Stillwater provides free Trap, Neuter & Return services for community cats in Stillwater and surrounding communities. They hold monthly clinics throughout the academic school year where each cat is examined, scanned for microchips, ear tipped, spayed or neutered, vaccinated (both rabies and FVRCP), and treated for parasites. Minor injuries are also addressed and treated.

In addition to providing the cats and community a great service, each clinic allows veterinary and pre-veterinary students to gain valuable learning experiences about quality, high volume spay and neuter.

It is a non-profit organization funded by Petco Foundation grants, OSU-CVHS, private donors and local businesses – all invaluable because, on average, it costs 30 dollars per cat to buy the supplies for the services that they provide.

Their mission is to reduce the homeless cat population through a no cost, high volume Trap Neuter & Return program for the community of Stillwater, Oklahoma and the surrounding areas.

Trap Neuter & Return (or TNR) is a humane method for addressing the ever growing feral and stray cat population within the United States. TNR works by sterilizing unowned and feral cats and then returning the cats to their original locations or colonies. While the ultimate goal is that the colony will cease to remain as the cats are unable to reproduce, there are many immediate benefits of TNR (for both human and cat!)

It is estimated that there are more unowned free-roaming cats within the US than there are owned pet cats. Adoption and rehoming of these cats is not always an option, as most of the unowned and free-roaming cats are born wild and are lacking proper human socialization. Without the required socialization skills, feral cats fear and do not trust humans.

At Operation Catnip, Stillwater, their program addresses the feral and stray cat population through spaying and neutering.

# Cats Protection (UK)

Today, Cats Protection is the UK's largest feline welfare charity. In the last 90 years, they have rehomed over 1.5 million cats and kittens and championed cat welfare. Their vision is a world where every cat is treated with kindness and an understanding of its needs.

It was founded in 1927 as the Cats Protection League by animal Welfare Campaigner, Jessey Wade.

In the 1950s, a legacy allowed them to open their first shelter. In the following decade, they launched their first neutering voucher scheme, called Cat Population Limitation.

They changed their name to Cats Protection in 1998, introducing a new logo and new branding. Today, they have more than 10,000 volunteers across the UK.

They have simple and clear objectives to help cats:
**Homing** - Finding good homes for cats in need.
**Neutering** - Supporting and encouraging the neutering of cats.
**Information** - Improving people's understanding of cats and their care.

# Battersea Dogs and Cats Home (UK)

Battersea is here for every dog and cat; and has been since 1860. They believe that every dog and cat deserves the best. That's why they help every dog and cat in need – whether it's newly born or getting on; cute, or cute in its own way.

From the moment they welcomed their first stray dog in 1860, they have been placing our animals at the center of everything they do. More than three million animals later, they're still working hard to achieve their vision that every dog and cat should live in a home where they are treated with love, care and respect.

Battersea aims to never turn away a dog or cat in need of help, caring for them until their owners or loving new homes can be found, no matter how long it takes. They are champions for, and supporters of, vulnerable dogs and cats, determined to create lasting changes for animals in our society.

They are one of just a few British animal rescue centers that run a non-selective intake policy. This means that they accept any breed of animal, at any age, including dogs or cats with serious medical and behavioral problems.

Their expert team of dog trainers and veterinary staff give the animals in their care the best possible chance of a fresh start in a happy new home.

They work hard to educate the public about responsible pet ownership including microchipping, neutering and training. This includes educational talks and visits to schools and organisations, events, and publications.

Everything that they do as individuals and teams, as vets and volunteers, fundraisers and foster carers, nurses, kennel and rehoming staff, is underpinned by their values:

- **Care** – They are passionate about the welfare of dogs and cats, and all their work is inspired by the needs of, and our love for, animals.

- **Excellence** – They have been working tirelessly to provide shelter for animals for over 160 years. They are one of the oldest animal charities in the world and the knowledge and experience we have gained has made them credible leaders in their field.

- **Determination** – They deal with some of the most challenging situations that impact the lives of dogs and cats. They seek to tackle problems at source by working actively with communities and wider society, challenging misconceptions and encouraging owners to take responsibility for their pets and treat animals humanely. They state quite definitely that they will not shy away from difficult issues.

- **Respect** – They promise to treat all animals and people with respect and dignity.

- **Integrity** – They are trustworthy. They are indebted to our supporters and greatly value all the donations given to them, ensuring they are carefully spent on providing the best possible future for animals.

- **Commitment** – Battersea strives to find every dog and cat a loving home. They put no limit on the time an animal stays with them, and we will never put an animal to sleep unless significant medical, safety or legal reasons compel them to do so.

## Additional Charities

Copies have also been distributed to a few other animal charities and vets around the world. If you have bought a copy from one of these, rest assured; they should have received a share of the profits as well.

Made in the USA
San Bernardino, CA
23 April 2019